Christopher Flowers
Flowers.christopher@gmail.com
www.flowersflix.com

ISBN-10: 0615522416
ISBN-13: 978-0615522418

Cover art by Michael Mercer and Christopher Flowers. Cover image taken in part from NASA via appropriate usage guidelines.

Salt of the Earth

a novel by

Christopher Flowers

PART ONE

Chapter 1

Orion stood, one foot propped on the Schultz converter, watching the quirky mechanism scrape permafrost from Europa's surface and convert it into drinkable water. The hair along his temples was cropped and gray; the purple scar on his cheek, which was almost regal, ached because of the ceaseless cold.

The Schultz completed its task and abandoned the weight of Orion's left leg, careening along the frozen surface in calculated patterns, tapping here and there with its tinny arm, searching for dislodged fragments of alien ice. Orion righted himself and checked his gauges. Soon he was trudging along the surface at a surprisingly brisk pace, the teeth of his boots gnawing at the frigid steppe, minuscule cracks spreading before him like rakes of lightning. Overhead, Jupiter swirled.

That was the one thing he didn't mind about the desiccate moon: the gasses of its anchor planet, writhing slowly in a deep palette of mauve and russet, converging and eventually dissipating as ghostly lovers. For the duration of his existence there he had enjoyed a spectacular view of "The Beast"—the Great Red Spot. Lately, though, it had begun to burrow into his subconscious. It was a splinter lodged just below the temporal cortex, scarcely evading removal, becoming more than a notable annoyance with each throbbing synapse.

In reality, he had become paranoid.

On Tuesday he had crossed paths with Tryson Pennington, self-designated Scuttlebug priest and all-around religious nut-job, whom always lunged at the opportunity to interrogate Orion regarding his conspicuous absence at the most recent communion.

"So, Ori," Tryson began, his green eyes focused through the slit in his visor. "We missed you on Sunday."

Sun-day. The word was painful for those who had survived, and a vote had been held early in The Expansion to permanently change the designation. Ultimately, though, it was decided that erasing it would somehow indicate that they were giving up on what was rightfully theirs. That would've been catastrophic. The most recent census reported the suicide rate as being eighty-one percent. Orion knew that was an optimistic figure.

"There is no Sunday" Orion muttered. "The Sun is gone. What's left there," he said, motioning to the weak flare dissolving on the horizon, "is a dead star." The priest laughed in his usual way, a short guttural bark. It generated grainy feedback.

"You know what I mean. Scuttlebug is all we have here—and all we need. He's supreme. You know that."

He turned to the dim line of gray hovels and research stations strewn across the icy hillside.

"This is important stuff we're doing, right? I mean, it's this or Pluto, and nobody wants Pluto. It's not even a moon. And what would we do there? Sit in our lawn chairs and watch *nothing*? Adjust the array so we could listen to *nothing*?"

"There's always Alpha Centauri," Orion said.

For a moment there was silence, and then the low, groaning shift of mile-thick ice. "Not in our lifetime, neighbor. And you can count me out of any 'practice runs' the Union has planned." Tryson suddenly appeared lost in thought.

"I don't know. If it comes down to it, and I'm sure it's the end, I guess I'd give it a shot. Why not?"

Orion wasn't sure. His visor swiveled upward, toward The Beast.

"Do you ever feel like God is watching?"

It was exactly the wrong question to ask, but before he could stop himself the words had clicked out of his mouth as if they were connected to some primitive reflex that he would never be able to suppress.

"Yes," Tryson said, "But I don't think God is on Jupiter."

"What if God *is* Jupiter?" Orion asked calmly. "What if The Beast is God? Look at it. It's an eye, and it never blinks. It's been staring us down since the moment we got here. It's like God is there—right *there*—and for the first time in tens of thousands of years we, us—humans—can actually see a part of Him peering through the veil. Aren't we supposed to look away or something? Shouldn't our bodies be imploding? Or exploding? Or turning into dust?"

Tryson's eyes flashed red in the rotating illumination screen. He smiled and walked away, a line of stars glowing like fireflies behind the awkward bulk of his helmet.

"Sunday," he said, "We all expect to see you on Sunday."

The Schultz came zipping up to where Orion stood, its narrow display flickering in the haze of dusk. It was true that there was oxygen present, but it wasn't much— only enough to last a few seconds with a cracked pane. Enough to send, perhaps, one final transmission.

He deciphered the garbled message—which slogged across the android's breast in an archaic font—and released a heavy sigh. It was time for his supplements.

Orion plodded back to his Korean issue home, a shallow construction that continuously bore its platinum foundation into the eastern rim of the plateau. He had decided several weeks earlier to fashion a mural on the broad side, just to make it a little more personal. As he approached the images of horses galloping across freshly cut meadows, nostrils dilating and hooves falling like hammers, he felt childish and idiotic. This endeavor had taken three days of his PTO. It looked like something that would have been airbrushed onto the spare wheel cover a late twentieth century conversion van. But that didn't matter. It reminded him of the stories his grandfather had told him about the days when Earth—the only real planet—still existed.

He often thought about the subway that had snaked its way beneath Manhattan; how the walls of each station (which were renovated, of course, during the Second Renaissance) were intricately pieced together with tile mosaics that depicted children prancing around cylindrical protrusions called "fire hydrants." There were also elderly women dragging poodles on chains, chattering gaily as they traversed the cracked sidewalks of Christopher Street. The crème de la crème, though, was the 121st Street Station, which featured a grimy, whiskey-lacquered rendition of the solar system.

"Each one was unique, you understand," his grandfather had explained, "and the artistry was brilliant. Simply brilliant. I never saw them, of course. But my great grandfather did."

Soon Orion found himself standing in the airlock, his vaccusuit bringing on the usual bout of claustrophobia. He squirmed when the door slammed behind him and the air rushed in. Once he was safely through the inner airlock, he said "Earth" as plainly and loudly as he could. A spinning image of the small blue planet as it had previously existed began to materialize in the center of the hovel, and Orion collapsed to the floor, fists planted squarely under his chin. He stared dreamily at the swirling pixels, as would a child on Christmas Eve in the midst of the cornucopia of gifts lining the trunk of a glittering Douglas fir.

This was his routine. Collect the samples that had been approved by the Schultz; speak to whichever neighbor had decided it was a nice day—or night, or whatever purgatory it was they inhabited—to go for a stroll in the eternal emptiness; then he would retreat to the sanctuary of this "home," completely utilitarian in all its unaesthetic glory.

This rumination made him feel a little better about the coarse artwork outside (which he would almost certainly be reprimanded for).

Ori switched off the thermal playback monitor that had been grafted to his undersuit. Its sole purpose was to record everything that unfolded on Europa so the Five Planet Union would have a clear understanding of how the researchers spent their time. The monitor could be linked to any holodeck, and Orion had been encouraged on several occasions by his supervisors—during their increasingly infrequent visits—to examine the footage for ways of maximizing productivity during his waking hours.

Of course, if he didn't review it, it didn't really matter. The video was automatically transferred to his console and sent to the Headquarters at Neptune. Whether he wanted them to or not, the Officials would see what he had been up to. As far as he knew, there was no way to disconnect the feed.

The Schultz soon emerged from its own doggy-door-sized entrance.

"Don't forget your report, sir," it said. "This is vital to the—"

"I know," Orion cut it off. "The existence and ever-expanding knowledge of the F.P.U."

"Log," Ori bellowed, "I went out at 9 a.m. And guess what? There was ice. Can you believe it? Ice! Oh yes, and the scuttlebugs, which haven't moved more than two miles in the past week. End report."

"Sir," the Schultz began, "You shouldn't..."

"Go away," Orion said softly, his eyes fixed on the revolving hologram. The Schultz scurried to its corner and quietly transformed itself into a small cube.

The idea that these giant mammals, which moved their bulk sluggishly in and out of the primordial stew that churned beneath his feet, represented some sort of hope for organic dark matter manipulation sickened him. They were merely over-sized slugs that, on occasion, had been theorized—*theorized*—to somehow inexplicably "teleport" themselves thousands of feet. It was thought that some had covered areas spanning hundreds of miles.

But proof was scarce.

All the F.P.U. had to go on were some garbled thermal readings of what they titled "instantaneous displacement events." This data had been acquired when

Europa was first colonized nearly a decade earlier. No real activity had occurred since that point, but Orion had been assigned to this utterly miserable outpost until "conclusive evidence" could be collected.

So far the *limax gigantus* hadn't done anything out of the ordinary.

They simply cut slow paths through the stolid permafrost, periodically wandering in and out of the Europan Sea at its base, feeding on bioluminescent organisms similar to phytoplankton and releasing pungent pheromones during the mating season. They were little more than intergalactic humpback whales.

"Alpha Centauri," Orion said to the computer. Earth disappeared in a flash of green and was replaced by the blinding star. "Dim," Orion said, "Zoom, QR-491."

The tiny planet emerged as a dark blip; it was hardly more than a mole drowning in the presence of Alpha Centauri's omnipotent radiation.

Its features became visible as the perpendicular holocams tightened their lenses, and soon Orion was viewing what he (and many others) believed to be salvation. All probes and satellites reported that its composition was virtually identical to his home planet's—80% nitrogen, 19% oxygen, 1% whatever-the-hell else.

QR-491's surface was also dotted with blue. Salt lakes, the passing satellites and Clonpulls had postulated, and there was one large ocean. And QR-491 looked warm.

It looked like home.

Or, at least, what he had always been taught home should look like.

There existed only one problem: it was inconceivably far away, and F.P.U. photon travel was in its infancy. But it was the only way any human would ever conquer the staggering distance (in his lifetime, at least).

Borsen's theory of re-assembled matter held up when it came to the ship and the lifeless metals and alloys it was constructed of. The first volunteers to test the engine weren't familiar with Borsen's theory, though. This was at the genesis of the Expansion. They were stragglers huddled together in a slum in Fulton Villa. They had been coerced to Mars with promises of breaking through the frontier and being the ones to "pave the way for humanity." They were also told that rent-free flats would be theirs upon return to Neptune. The broadcasts called it "Clearing the Path!"

Not surprisingly, the tests were unsuccessful, and the ill-fated voyagers had once again become part of the antediluvian smorgasbord that is interstellar space; molecules and bits of debris endlessly tumbling from one end of creation to the other until they collided with *something*.

Wash. Rinse. Repeat.

Orion, however, was familiar with Borsen's theory. He had studied it thoroughly via the F.P.U. broadcasts while seated in the center of his living room floor. He wanted desperately for the Union engineers to unlock the secret—to crack the code and discover the way that flesh, blood, bones and soul could make the trip without being dismantled by the singularity. They were on the verge—"The Brink!"—day after day, decade after decade, the solution was dangled in front of the survivors like a dirty carrot. So close, so tangible, and so unattainable.

If there were even a kernel of truth to the claims, "that's good," Orion thought, because The Beast would undoubtedly remain fixed on him for months—perhaps years—to come. And he knew he couldn't take that. Between Tryson's badgering him to go with the other researchers to church and worship the almighty Scuttlebug and Jupiter bearing down on him, he would lose it.

Snap.

And, he realized, it would probably all take place in the form of him smashing another researcher's air-generator into extra-lunar powder. He also wouldn't be able to resist the temptation to empty the greasy innards of some poor Schultz that crossed his path at precisely the wrong time. He would "grip it and rip it," as his grandfather had said. Orion imagined that the cornered researcher would have no choice but to retreat into his vaccusuit like a frightened turtle.

Then he would wait.

Both Orion and his victim would wait for the inevitable. And when it came, it would be a release: from The Beast, from Tryson, from Scuttlebug—from *everything*. A bitterly cold explosion of the lungs. A hardening of the veins.

The release.

Chapter 2

Carla Grayson was not attractive. Her frame was gaunt and ashy, her cheeks sunken and hard. She had been sentenced, centuries before her conception, to live out her existence on the Pluto-Charon resonance. That's the way the Union worked when it came to Carla and her ancestors. They paid for the sins of their fathers.

Friar Grayson (Carla's great, great, great grandfather) and Stephen Pynchon played integral roles in the destruction of the solar system. At a time when the world was dependent on fossil fuels, which were almost completely depleted, they conjured up a miracle: the Pynchon Orbiter.

Friar had discovered, deep within the Martian polar basin, alloys that could withstand the searing heat of a near-Sun orbit. Solar power, *real* solar power, was stripped from the star's hydrogen core in hundred thousand-mile long bands and compressed into mammoth, gleaming photonicity cells. It was a seemingly endless supply that would last as long as the Sun burned. The best part was that the process only extracted miniscule (what would later be referred to as a "relative" term) amounts of the crucial element. Each cell generated enough electricity for the entire planet to operate for five consecutive years.

Stars, as was previously unknown until that point in the late 22nd century, are relatively unstable bodies. The Pynchon's ceaseless plucking—month after month, year after year—eventually took its toll. It seemed that the governments, as they existed in pre-Expansion history, thought it best to harvest as many cells as possible; that it would be best to store them in the cavernous underground facilities.

"To secure the future!"

Many said (and still say) the disaster could've been prevented if only one cell had been taken every decade. By the time that theory had been published, though, it was too late.

Like a slowing top, the star began to wobble. Soon it was an unraveling ball of cosmic yarn, its fiery threads flailing like the gargantuan tentacles of a nuclear squid. It seemed to be fabricating a hellish garment that was fit for only Satan himself.

What should've taken billions of years was accomplished in less than fifty. A premature red giant emerged, its blood-colored bulk bearing down on Earth, bathing everything in the stoplight glow of crimson radiation. Earth's atmosphere peeled away—ironically—in the fashion of dead skin after a sunburn.

Humans fled as if they were the inhabitants of an anthill that had been gouged by the splintered twig of a five-year old. Those that survived eventually found solace in something completely unexpected: a miracle mineral congealing in our own celestial backyard.

Philidium, an entirely new element discovered on Pluto, was a key piece of the puzzle in solving Borsen's theory of photon travel for organics. And the F.P.U. made sure that Carla Grayson paid her debt to mankind by playing an integral role in the mining of the volatile substance, just as her ancestors had. When she had children—a certainty—they would also be born into servitude. The Grayson family had become the sole scapegoat in the Pynchon Extinction Event, and that was accepted. A lingering hatred for the Grayson name burned in those who were educated; those with direct ties to the Union.

That's how Carla came to reside on Pluto. Back bent, feet planted among jagged bedrock, she mined the deposits with the rigidity of something mechanical. Her form was broken and hollow.

Carla's only companions were a smattering of rough and tumble inmates.

But there was hope. The outpost was at a turning point. After decades of being subjected to the barbarity of the F.P.U. and something akin to space-age slavery, the static of rebellion had begun to fill the vacuum. The convicts had finally built up the nerve to storm the typically undermanned supply vessel and escape; to seek refuge on Io, Pangea, or even Europa, with its supply of water (100% *all-natural* water, the prisoners whispered eagerly) that didn't taste like plastic and didn't culminate in dysentery.

Carla leaned over the hole she had hewn and extracted the philidium in amorphous globs, the plasma-like substance congealing noiselessly in vats operated by the Shultz. It reminded her of an opal, the way it shone iridescent when tilted toward the pink glow of the distant Sun. She wondered how it powered the device that depended on it—the engine that had put Clonpulls into orbit around QR-491, detailing the planet's features and beaming back data, waiting patiently for the rest of civilization to join the party.

Samuel Farragut approached Carla alongside with Chiu Mate, and, as they stepped gingerly over the grinning crevices of a burgandy floe, Carla knew what was imminent.

"Today is the d-d-day," Chiu said, her excitement flaring the stutter. "The s-s-ship will be here at fourteen h-h-hundred. Just enough time."

"Yeah, *just* barely enough," Samuel blurted.

"Have you told the others?" Carla asked.

"No," Chiu whispered, turning down her volume, "I was going to tell W-W-Willy, but he seems anxious. Ya know? He's itchin', or something. They have the desire, but not the b-b-backbone. We can't trust them. It'll just be us."

"It's settled, then," Carla murmured.

Her stomach roiled.

It was already thirteen fifty-one, and the thought of leaving the most forlorn penal colony in the system and reaching Europa, the moon that could very well be the next great epicenter of humanity, thrilled her to the marrow. She shivered and motioned to Samuel.

"Are you sure you're ready?"

Sam knocked on the plexifab of his visor and nodded.

"It'll be a cakewalk," he said, "Just keep them busy."

Their steadfast anticipation slowly melted into gooey enthusiasm as one hour passed.

Then two.

Just as the plan was about to be abandoned and reassessed, a moving light appeared above the hemline of an obscure canyon, inching forward steadily. Soon, engines fired perfunctorily as the beacon took the comically ovoid shape of an F.P.U. transport. The ineluctable nature of the situation caused a cold wave of panic to crest on Carla, but Chiu and Samuel appeared resolute.

The craft landed eerily, as it always did—as *everything* did—without a sound, limbs extending rapidly and puncturing the scintillating powder that glazed the tundra. A hatch opened and two guards with Jovian release-stunners emerged.

What had been a wave transformed into a rollicking tsunami, and Carla lost control. She felt it happening, but was powerless to stop it. Her malnourished arms tingled and acid rose in her throat. She crumpled, regurgitated what remained of her supplements, and fell to the ground.

Samuel and Chiu exchanged nervous glances. The plan, which they had approached Carla with months earlier and honed into a full-fledged conspiracy to bring down the system, had suddenly fallen apart at the seams like a moth-eaten sweater. Their meticulously discussed and rehearsed decision to fake a leak in Samuel's suit—to feign exposure, to roll-over in convulsions and finally be carried back to the dormitory one mile away (an appropriate distance from the ship and everyone else) was on the verge of ruin. The trio had wanted to lure the guards inside, recover one of their stunners and confiscate the official Union vaccusuits. No one would've expected it. And, when the other prisoners finally discovered the truth—found the nude government employees bound and issuing threats—it would be far too late.

Samuel had also decided to trap a guard in the airlock and watch him scream and pound the massive door. He had kept this to himself.

The guards rushed to Carla's side, kneeling and barking orders at her vacuusuit's computer. The other prisoners looked up in surprise, their drills powering down and every available Schultz asking how it could be of assistance.

Samuel and Chiu had come to the conclusion that they would leave Pluto or die trying. It was that simple. Carla, revolutions aside, just wanted to see something else. She had been a creature at the fringe of existence her entire life. Now, at age forty, it seemed a vivid inevitability that she would meet her end on a far-flung Kuiper object. The vague realization that the world she now occupied was inching ever closer to oblivion as the slack in its invisible tether gradually lengthened finally spurred her to action.

The guards debated what to do with the fallen celebrity. They eventually picked her up and started to carry her to the dormitory. They breathed heavily into their microphones and called for everyone to keep working and remain where they were.

Samuel licked his lips, and the blood flaring the capillaries in his cheeks made him twitch.

He sprung the trap before the officers had left the mining district.

Farragut shoved one guard to the ground and stomped on his visor; the static from his suit caused all involved to wince, instinctively scrambling to reduce volume. The stunner she—*a woman*, Sam realized, feeling the contours of her suit—had carried was loose. It slid down a granulated crag and came to rest in the pitch dimple left by the impact of a small meteorite.

Every other prisoner dropped their drills and lumbered among the rocks dumbly, eventually making their way toward the dormitory as a panicked herd. The unified rebellion that Chiu had imagined wasn't in the cards. If a stray bolt from a stunner managed to make contact with the CPU of a vacuusuit (which was located, conveniently enough, mid-chest) the whole thing would rupture. This, it seemed, was motivation enough to flee the scene.

Another guard emerged from the open airlock of the supply ship. He descended the circular ladder quickly. His eyes were glassy and red—adrenaline rendered him superhuman.

He had beaten Samuel.

Picking up the stunner, he fired a single shot. It struck Sam's visor, which shattered and swirled a Dandelion spore ballet that quickly vanished into one of Pluto's many wounds.

The skin on his face became taut and he clutched at his throat. Farragut collapsed and continued his plunge down the hill as would a rag doll, rolling to a stop at his murderer's boots.

The Union guard went Armstrong-hopping across the surface toward the ship, screaming frantically for backup.

The remaining guard, which Samuel had successfully disabled, was unconscious. Chiu dragged him roughly across the scarred landscape toward the dormitory. Carla's breathing began to slow as she surveyed the aftermath of the attack.

She wasn't upset over Samuel's death. He was a manipulator, like a dozen other greedy and self-righteous rogues she'd encountered. His absence would make reaching Europa that much easier, in fact, because he would have made every effort to ditch his comrades on a passing asteroid just so he could make it to the government center and civilization edifice orbiting Neptune all by his lonesome. With the proper skull augmentation, she had no doubt he would've blended into the throngs scouring the markets for synthetic fruit.

Carla quickly caught up with Chiu, her visor fogged from panicked breaths, and picked up the unconscious guard's legs. They soon had her at the dormitory entryway. There they worked swiftly, stripping the woman down to her thermal undersuit and stuffing her into a closet.

The delirious Union guard started to babble.

Alarmed, Chiu struck her across the scalp with a wrench. She moaned and sunk into the pile of laundry at the base of the storage compartment.

"Jesus," she said softly. "She's a woman." Blood flowed from behind the guard's left ear in a heavy stream.

"New plan," Chiu said quickly. "You put on her vacuusuit. I'll be the prisoner. They'll recognize you, but not if you put your visor down and set the tint. And change the way you walk. Add a limp or something." Chiu paused, then inhaled. "A woman. I can't believe it. How lucky are we?"

Carla dressed clumsily. Even though the previous owner of the outfit in question was of the same gender, it was much too large, and she lumbered across the open area of the dormitory like a drunken sasquatch, her arms outstretched for added effect. The warm blood kissed the nape of her neck, and she squeezed her eyes in a vain attempt to block the sensation.

Chiu put on a pair of restraints that the guard had stuffed into her belt. They looked at each other briefly and moved out of the dormitory.

Three other F.P.U. Officials had emerged from the ship, and were sprinting (as best they could) towards the pair of felons.

"This is the one that tried to kill Spivey," Carla said, lowering her voice slightly and glancing at the name sewn into the front of the vacuusuit of the still-panicked guard.

"Then what the hell did that one do?" a man named Ashbury said, pointing to Samuel, still crumpled in a heap at the bottom of the slope.

"The dead one," Carla said, "tried to rush me. They would've killed me. *He* would've killed me," she said, wagging a finger at Sam, "But this one interceded. She picked up a rock. Said she wanted to finish him. She was going to try to crush his visor. Beat it in."

Ashbury eyed Chiu carefully. Medics had emerged from the ship and were tending to Spivey, helping him back toward the hatch, telling him that he had just experienced severe psychological trauma and that his mind and body needed rest. Their suits shone, clean and prim. They looked like ghosts.

"All right, fine," the official said. "Let's get this cleaned up. I'll be filling out reports for the next three months." In a tired voice, he ordered them to move the equipment back to the ship.

Carla escorted Chiu into the exposed dock, where the other Officials were unloading rations and a new converter. They hauled the large containers out onto the edge of the hatch and watched them fall slowly to the dusty plane below, scattering pebbles with each buoyant, exaggerated bounce.

Chiu was secured in her seat. Carla jammed the barrel of a stunner into her visor. She maintained that position and scanned the bridge, plotting her next move with as much composure and tenacity as she could muster.

Then she saw it.

There, adjacent to the aft airlock, was a rack loaded with F.P.U. weaponry. And not just stunners; high caliber rifles were stacked seven deep next to chain guns (good, old-fashioned automatic weapons that fired with or without the presence of air). In fact, just about every kind of instrument of death was at her disposal.

Still, they couldn't just start unloading on everyone while the ship made its way to the Union station on autopilot; if they did, they would likely crack the pressure seal with a stray shot and come in contact with the void.

They would end up like Samuel and countless others.

Carla reduced the tint on her visor and looked at Chiu. She nodded toward the rack.

Chiu peered over her shoulder and understood. If they were going to do it, they had to do it now. The ship's engines rumbled to life and a cloud of powder wafted in front of the solar shield. There were still four Officials on the surface. Carla peered out of the hatch and saw them trotting back toward the ship.

Casually, she stepped up to the rack and removed a chain gun. One of the pilots stood, clapped his gloved hands, and surveyed the surface from the cusp of the open airlock. Carla shouldered her weapon and approached the man.

She kicked him in the small of his back as hard as she could.

He fell headfirst onto the rocks below. Shouting and stiff orders arose over her earpiece.

There wasn't enough time to locate the release code for the restraints so Chiu could pick up a spare weapon and join the fray.

Carla squeezed the trigger and a round tore through the now scrambling co-pilot's chest. The man's suit erupted in flames.

Carla dragged his infernal mass to the open door and heaved it overboard. The one remaining official tackled her from behind, causing the chain gun to skip awkwardly across the grated floor. The four Officials outside scaled the ladder leading up to the hatch with speed and efficiency. In what seemed to be the most logical decision, Carla did the only thing she could. She moved to the nav-system panel, punched the large green display, and braced herself as a blast rose from the thrusters. The ship trembled and was instantly catapulted from the desolate dwarf planet.

The guard still on board grasped Carla's helmet from behind and began repeatedly smashing it against the eroded transom.

It was pointless. This was the durable stuff; genuine plexifab.

Carla managed to get to her knees and deliver an elbow to his gut, giving her just enough leeway to shimmy free. Clutching at the nearby weapon rack, she retrieved a machine gun, its stocky butt bulbous at her shoulder, training it on him as he rose to his feet. The cabin still wasn't pressurized. The exposed hatch was a gateway to hell.

"You have to get off," she said coldly.

"No," he said, "I won't go that way. Besides, you can't fire that now. There's no air."

She fired a single shot past him. He froze.

"Look, you know what it means if I go out there. Let me off at a colony. Somewhere. Please. Not *here*."

"If you go now you can still reach the others. Your suit has boosters."

"It's too far." He paused. "I can't make it. It's too far."

Carla looked beyond the solar shield and saw the surface of Pluto becoming an intricate diorama of dark lines and overlapping craters.

"Get off now or I'll rupture your suit."

The official's eyes darted between Carla and Chiu, who sat in silence.

He charged.

Carla fired several shots into his abdomen. The official reeled backward, through the oval hatch, a trail of opaque gas trailing thinly like cigarette smoke. The two of them watched as he blended with the winking stars.

He looked like a comet.

Chapter 3

At the mouth of the Temple of Scuttlebug, Orion wondered why he hadn't visited the place since his arrival on this moon. Every other researcher spent their moments not collecting samples chiseling away at the hulking ice sculpture that constituted the steeple. It was an eerily detailed depiction of a scuttlebug. The animal's tusks scythed skyward from under a cleft lip. Poised like a charmed cobra, the cloudy monument kept vigil over everything that transpired on Europan Research Station AA.

The entire church had, in fact, been carved out of a glacial remnant. The pews were smooth and crystallized, aligned with geometric perfection before a pulpit that maintained a perpetual diamond glow.

Orion nodded courteously to each colonist when he entered the sanctuary. They murmured excitedly at the prospect of a new convert.

Tryson approached the pulpit bulkily, his vacuusuit's weight causing him to move with slow, calculated steps. Opening the *Book of Scuttle*, he began to read slowly, a solemn timbre commanding each disciple to cease his or her chatter.

"We all know that Scuttlebug is the answer to our problems," he began. "*Every* problem we might encounter, even. He is our salvation from this galaxy, which is void and empty of any place that we may call home. Aside from 'algae'" he said, using a centuries old word that drew snickers from some adolescents on the front row, "Scuttlebug is the only complex being—aside from ourselves, of course—that is still alive in this system.

"And what does this tell us about *our* survival? What can we expect to happen in the next ten years? Twenty? Thirty? One hundred? The answers, my friends, will come from Him. 'Instantaneous teleportation,' as our forefathers called it, is a reality. Scuttlebug has the key to its secrets. That is His gift to us."

The congregation applauded mutely.

"And today we have a guest," Tryson said, nodding to Ori. "Mr. Orion Esocrat, a newcomer who has, for his own reasons, remained absent from our ceremonies these many months. But, due to Scuttlebug's will, he is present today. Welcome, brother."

At Pennington's cue, every person in the frozen church stood and made their way toward Orion. They shook his hand eagerly, raising their visors so he could see the joy on their chapped faces. He returned a conservative smile. As the line thinned, he took a moment to peer through the diaphanous ceiling.

Through the fog of hewn ice, the Beast continued to stare.

Ori merely endured the remainder of the service. There were several moments where he thought he would vomit in his vacuusuit and have to deal with the putrid stench of partially digested rations until he was able to return home and complete the detox procedure. Watching the attendees rest oval helmets against the backs of pews, he came to a nauseating comprehension as to what his time on Europa would ultimately lead to.

Insanity.

The majority of the researchers that lived here had done their work diligently and without complaint for years, but now they worshiped an extra-terrestrial worm.

That's what the solar system had come to.

And this "religion" had spread like a plague across moons, planets and space stations; each person that came into contact with this idea of the "Savior Scuttlebug" became wholly infected until they, at some point in their lives, made the pilgrimage—often without documentation—to the mecca that had been constructed by the truly faithful. Orion believed he was one of the few that truly grasped the lunacy of it all.

What had happened to the God of our fathers—the 'Christians' that had lived so long ago? He wondered about this frequently, though it had occurred to him that they were likely no different than the people currently kneeling at the chilled altar—babbling incessantly and clutching at crude idols.

Still, he couldn't ignore the rumors that persisted; that there were those concealing their knowledge of a true God—a "Jehova"—that would one day return in a maelstrom of light and manna, peeling back the clouds as if they were the husk of a divine fruit, and incomprehensible splendor.

But *what* clouds? The only clouds that existed were the shrouds of the gas giants and their satellites, and they did little more than scald lungs and generate scorching rain.

This was where his train of thought always derailed.

It made no sense, this worship of Scuttlebug, but Orion took pity on those that believed it (or "He") was the solution to the woes of the universe.

Because, really, what else was there?

His own solutions were much more rational; much more scientific.

Borsen's theory was the best he had—because to him, and apparently a significant contingency of Union Officials, it made sense. The Scuttlebug followers believed in it too, but for entirely different reasons.

"Wrong reasons," Ori surmised.

So he tried to remain sensible. If the Clonpulls had really been delivered to QR-491, then, he deduced, there must be a way for living, breathing people to reach it. Standard propulsion would stretch the journey to an estimated thirteen years. To Orion, thirteen years wasn't much in the grand scheme of things. But to become a part of such a journey—which would almost certainly be in the works—one needed credentials; connections: some sort of measurable influence.

Even though this was, in all probability, more myth than reality, the thought caused him to wander out of the cavernous hall just as Tryson was wrapping up his sermon on the origins of the philosophers who had discovered that God is Scuttlebug. Orion took his time returning to his meager abode. He absorbed Jupiter's glower as it pulsed in the sky like an electric marble.

He had become so tangled in thought that he hardly noticed the pair of thrusters firing in the distance, low over the potted surface.

When Ori had gathered his senses, he realized it wasn't the right time of week for an F.P.U. supply craft to be delivering a shipment.

He wondered if something was wrong—if there was some sort of emergency. "Perhaps," he thought with dread, "another expansion." Acid rose in his throat.

Yet another evacuation.

*   *   *

After releasing Chiu from the straps of the holding chair, Carla pressurized the cabin and initiated the ship's artificial gravity drive. She removed her helmet and peered over the sill of the porthole, watching the resonance sink into the gulf.

The standard trajectory of return for an F.P.U. supply ship would take them, in an elliptical arc, to the government complex orbiting Neptune.

Carla quickly deactivated the autopilot and instructed the nav-system to take them on a direct course to Europa.

There, she believed they would find refuge in at least one of the research colonies, which were thought to be sympathetic toward fugitives because of their newfound faith.

"You didn't have to kill him, you know," Chiu said in a half-whisper. For a moment, Carla pretended like she hadn't heard. She crossed her arms and sank into the nylon cushioning of the Captain's chair. Greasy locks uncoiled when she removed her helmet.

"What was I supposed to do?" she whispered. "What would we have done with him on Europa? Convinced him to become a colonist? Told him to keep our little escapade back on Pluto under wraps, because, you know, it could get out and give us bad publicity?"

Chiu frowned and massaged the freckles spanning the bridge of her nose.

"He had enough air to make it back to the camp. He was just stubborn. It would've only taken a couple of hours."

But it didn't matter now. He was dead, and they were on the run. There was no doubt that the Officials abandoned at the philidium mines had already sent a transmission back to the Neptune Headquarters and told them to expect their ship to be arriving with two malnourished fugitives onboard.

That's what Carla hoped, anyway. She was counting on mistakes.

The prisoners being steadily transported on and off Pluto had helped foster a thorough understanding regarding the inner workings of the F.P.U., because, after all, the majority of criminals they arrested had served on the station at Neptune at some point (even if only for a week).

The bulk had committed minor offenses: abandoning their posts to try and get a glimpse of the philidium-fueled engine that would be the ultimate salvation of humanity; slipping out for a taste of Twilight; things of that sort.

Carla was sure that those who had learned any real information were promptly executed. They were probably flushed out of an airlock and chalked up to the increasingly more frequent deep space breakdowns that ended in the crew of a particular ship going bananas and deciding to take an unencumbered stroll in the everlasting nothing.

This is what most of her time spent drilling consisted of: conjecturing about what was really going on behind the scenes with the Union. She also devoted time to deliberating what it would take for her to abolish the slavery her family had been subject to for over half a millennium.

Despite the many tangents it embraced, Carla's mind always seemed to come back to one burning question: that of the validity of Borsen's theory. Was there any credence to it? Or was it something invented to give hope to a civilization on the brink of annihilation?

Many prisoners had told her the engine was real. The recent ones told her it was near completion.

She realized they could've been fakes—implants—sent to penetrate and infect the underground collective of ideals. Excitement and, more importantly, genuine *hope* radiating from their countenances had convinced her otherwise.

From what she had pieced together from the ones assigned tasks related to the fabled device (such as constructing the dark matter resistant innards that held the thing together) she was relatively sure that the ship was designed to conform its hull to the singularity that would carry it. Electromagnetic restraints had been fitted on each plug and a photon-fusion generator was at its core—this, she hypothesized, would prevent the engine from halting the biological functions of its passengers when the event horizon was breached.

It was said that testing had been done on animals; they were rocketed from Neptune to Pangea—the solar system's outermost giant—and back in less than a microsecond. The most current statistics were an improvement, as only 73% of kangaroos on board had returned without appendages (these sorts of statistics were delivered with sheepish grins).

Carla's attention was briefly captured by the sight of Chiu extracting a pillow from an overhead compartment, and then she began to drift with the ship.

She lay on the stiff carpet in front of the porthole, embracing the warmth that radiated from the thrusters below. Eventually Carla was enveloped by the heavy blanket of phasic REM, and her consciousness ambled along the corridor of vague tales passed down by her family—a family that would, as long as the F.P.U. existed, be forever incarcerated.

Carla's mother had told her about a species that was once abundant on Earth—something called a "dog." She had never seen a sim-vid of one, but had heard that the Rovers were their descendants. They generally had floppy ears and wet noses. Also, they were quadrupeds. She concocted an image of a "dog," the creature's (most likely) nimble legs gingerly cresting the sprawling dune of a Martian desert.

Soon she was at the place where Friar's wife had made scrambled eggs, a gelatinous food, which was prepared under the shade of an adobe hut that straddled a valley, every morning before the Sun rose above Olympus Mons.

A man approached the place, breathing heavily, a bundle of balloons trailing, his nose bright, red, and perfectly round.

He was terrifying.

The dog growled and was abruptly liquefied, becoming a metallic puddle that rippled in the gusts of an oncoming sandstorm. Peals of thunder shook the mountainside. The clown collected his money and left. Friar was a rich man, and it was a good thing; clowns weren't cheap, and his daughter's birthday would have to be postponed.

Martian sandstorms were violent, unpredictable events.

They were not to be taken lightly.

Chapter 4

Orion watched as the supply ship descended, its thrusters carving narrow trenches in the blue frost.

Looking over his shoulder, he saw that none of the congregation had noticed the untimely arrival of the rations. They were all still seated, heads pressed tightly against pews, absorbing the life-altering message that only Scuttlebug can deliver.

A flat realization that the ship had failed to land in the regulated zone, near the colony's border, caused Orion to take several steps back.

Something wasn't right.

His suspicion of an evacuation was rekindled. Once again Ori was certain that the Sun had decided to expand its waistline by a couple of million more miles that afternoon, and that Europa was no longer at minimum safe distance. Though this phase would not have been predicted, it wouldn't have been completely unexpected. Oddly, his dread was soon replaced with a calm acceptance, and the cool sweat coating his palms begin to feel less like the residue of some heated internal conflict and more like a soothing balm that reminded him—with welcome finality—that it was all beyond his control.

He had had to move all of his things a total of five times in his life—one more couldn't hurt, and, if he were to be frank with the Officials, he wasn't particularly fond of this place anyway.

Still, it meant more work. He sighed and began making his way back to his home, exhausted at the idea of once again jamming everything he owned into the large, air-tight container that had weathered so many long, cold trips across the chasm of outer system space.

When the hatch opened and he saw that there was only one F.P.U. Official accompanied by a civilian he felt himself begin to breathe. If this were an evacuation there would be a swarm of twenty men pouring from the tiny opening like fire ants from a freshly gouged mound, each sounding a cacophony of alarms and screaming for visors to be lowered and plexitex to be applied as quickly as possible.

The visitors approached Orion calmly, hands extended. They darkened their visors as they drew near, and almost vanished in the eerie morning glow emanating from the planet overhead.

"Hi," the F.P.U. official said, "I'm Beanca." Orion smiled and shook hands with the woman, just able to discern her pale features. He was able to determine, however, that her smile wasn't a broad one—it was reserved, not too generous.

Most colony ambassadors introduced themselves by identifying their outpost assignment and country of origin (traced back, of course, through Earth centuries and the information they had pieced together from genealogies, a surprising number of which had survived the Martian consumption some four hundred years earlier).

"I'm Orion," he said. "Orion Esocrat. Welcome to Europa Research Colony AA. I've never seen you guys out this way on a Sunday before. Everything okay? Big Red didn't decide to eat another planet, did it?" He laughed at his own joke, though the two women made no sound at all. Orion was sure the person not in an F.P.U. uniform was also a woman. It was her posture. Not rigid like a man's, but more unassuming. Fluid. Refined.

"I'm Liza," the other finally said, "And we've just had a long trip. I mean a really long trip—all the way from Pluto." Orion shuddered at the thought.

"Yeah," she perceived his disgust, "It's a hell hole. It shouldn't even be allowed to support bios."

"Tell me about it," Ori responded. "I served a rotation there a long time ago. I'll never go back," he said, eyeing them sternly.

He was cautious, but enjoyed the conversation he was having with the two women because it seemed authentic. There weren't any forced pleasantries such as those he encountered on a daily basis in his dealings with Tryson and the other members of the Scuttlebug faction. For the first time in what seemed an infinite purgatory he felt as if he could actually open up; that he could communicate with these people and divulge what was really on his mind. He found it a strange sensation.

It wasn't long before Orion noticed the reflection of The Beast in their visors. It stared him down even then, and, at that instant, managed to drive a devastating spike of truth directly through his cerebral cortex.

These people weren't from the F.P.U.

He should've noticed that right from the start, the way they emerged from the supply ship, their hands resting lazily on the seal of the hatch, their helmets instinctively jerking quickly from one side to another as they tried to ingest the environment as would a newly hatched chick.

F.P.U. Officials weren't like that. They were more militarized; more exacting, purpose-driven.

They moved in unison.

A large part of him wanted to sound his own alarm and contact the *real* F.P.U., to let them know that one of their billion dollar ships had been commandeered by... whom? Or—infinitely more terrifying—what? Rumors had circulated that foreign intelligences—creatures from beyond Pangea—had already infiltrated the ranks of the Union. He viewed this as ludicrous, but he wasn't in the mood for taking chances.

A deep and concentrated fear that the worship of Scuttlebug was just such a manifestation of an invasion, a glaring indication that an incursion would soon take place, had rooted itself in Orion's bowels. The unmistakable feeling that mankind had been encroaching on territory that wasn't theirs—and never would be—had plagued Ori for years. He mostly chalked this up to paranoia. The erratic behavior of his fellow researchers, though, hadn't helped settle the blossoming anxieties.

And now here were these two, landing an F.P.U. supply ship recklessly in the heart of the primary Europan research colony. How could two women, alone and without weapons, have taken control of a Union ship? The notion in and of itself was preposterous, but they stood before him, more tangible than Jupiter itself, basking in the presence of The Beast and staring Orion (he assumed) directly in his unshielded eyes.

The tint. Why did they do that? The sun was weak and low. It was completely unnecessary. This concealment converted any floundering sense of fear into a pitted metal ball whose weight caused his stomach to sag.

There was a twenty-year old stunner in the storage unit attached to his hut. His legs twitched at the thought of making a run for it and snapping up the weapon.

He wondered if he had the precision to land two bolts squarely against their vaccusuit processors before they could contaminate the colony and use it as a base to study his species and decide how best to eradicate it—to prevent homo sapiens from planting a large flag with an "H" in the center of non-Milky Way space.

"So," Beanca said, "Do you have any food here? I know you do. We're starving. The last time I had any supplements was three days ago."

"Why were you on Pluto?"

Orion asked the question with a firmness he hadn't intended, and the women stiffened.

"Food," Liza repeated, "We're hungry, Orion. Surely you won't keep us standing out here while you've got perfectly good supplements just sitting in your kitchen."

Orion froze, unable to speak. He only stared at them, wishing he had the strength necessary to reach the panel on his chest and return their darkened gaze.

"We were on Pluto because my father landed there to keep the prisoners in line," Beanca finally interjected. "He was a corrections officer. Neptune-class. Several of them—the prisoners—had decided to try and overtake a supply ship." She paused and let her head bob in contemplation. "One of them—the prisoners, I mean—got his hands on a chain gun and killed Roland. My father."

"Why did he have a chain gun? I've never heard of them sending corrections officers to Pluto—"

"Listen!" Liza barked angrily. "Her father was just murdered by an outpost felon. A person who didn't believe in the cause of the F.P.U.—someone wholly set against the goal of securing a habitable planet for us—*me* and *you*," she said, stabbing the emptiness with a hooked finger. "He died in the line of duty." Liza put her arm over Beanca's shoulder.

"The F.P.U. station at Neptune is dealing with solar flares, so we can't dock for a few more days. They authorized our diversion here; to this Scuttlebug-forsaken ice cube. We tried to be cordial, but you seem to question your fellow man—er, woman— for no good reason. I hate to be blunt, but please, let us have just a portion of your supplements and we'll be gone as soon as Headquarters gives the go-ahead for docking."

Orion fidgeted with the utility pouches on the right arm of his vacuusuit. They were obviously lying. But it didn't matter. He didn't have any other choice.

"I'm sorry," he said in the most cheerful voice he could muster, "My hovel is just over that glacier. Follow me."

*   *   *

Peering through the window of his cabin at the F.P.U. complex, Dr. Eugene Silvagno examined his fingers against the backdrop of the blue planet. They looked like a bramble of gnarled roots. He cracked his knuckles and drew in a deep breath. Silvagno allowed the air just enough time to mingle with the most intimate parts of his lungs before exhaling.

It felt good.

Standing, he did his best to smooth the wrinkles from the seat of his trousers and exited the room. The corridor was long and dotted with soft lights. Passing a woman in a tight purple suit, he smiled and lowered his head. The company of other humans was something he had sorely missed.

Having just returned from the first successful manned mission to QR-491, he had grown weary of deep space. The trip had taken almost a full decade: long enough for Silvagno to constantly quiz himself as to whether or not he had really retained all of the sanity he had originally exited the solar system with.

As he walked his mind wandered, in and out of the patterns of stars that he watched pass like approaching headlights on a dark road, around (and possibly through) large blurs that could have been—and were, in all probability—sprawling nebulae. The solitude combined with his steady diet of supplements and recycled urine had made him contemplate suicide more than once: much more than once, in fact. And now here he was, walking down a corridor, built by *people*, filled with artificial light and warm faces, his senses telling him all of it was real and that he had actually survived. Still, Eugene had the inclination that his mind would be forever petrified, perpetually tumbling forward against the resistance of... nothing.

Space.

The thought of its infinite cruelty made his throat tighten as he passed a robust fellow with jowls that trembled viciously with each step.

Then there was the secrecy.

The fact that he could tell no one where he was going, or why he was leaving, had crushed his soul. Eugene wasn't the most amicable person, but there were people he cared about. He was a rarity in that he had identifiable kin. For the doctor, the worst part was that the projection had been completely inaccurate; it wasn't eight years—it was almost ten. He was sure his family had designated him another poor sap taken in by the Union as a guinea pig for an experiment that ultimately would not provide a concrete answer to the puzzle of how, exactly, humanity might survive.

But it really *had* provided an answer, he ruminated proudly. This, above everything else, surprised even him. When recruited, he saw himself as anything but naïve; the risks were apparent, but they were worth it. In time, though, he realized he was *more* than naïve. He was hopeful—a word he considered synonymous with gullible.

Dr. Silvagno had expected to die before reaching QR-491. That's why he had signed up for the trip in the first place. In his mind the human race would never find a planet to inhabit—not in his lifetime, anyway—so he figured, "What the hell? At least I might get a chance to see something different. I'll lose it and be stuck, quite literally, in the middle of nowhere, just as miserable and destitute as before. But maybe I'll succeed. Maybe I'll make it to that place; that oasis, light years from all other possibilities. And then I'll save my species."

Silvagno frowned. He *was* naïve.

The good doctor was on the verge of entering a boardroom full of men in business attire, waiting eagerly for his report and full account of 491. There was still a part of him that wished he hadn't made it back. They had sponsored and funded this Borsen project, and they wanted facts—data; hard evidence that this planet could be populated following a migration of Biblical proportions.

He didn't have much for them. A few sim-vids, clips of the little blue-green anomaly, just like the ones the Clonpulls had sent years before, and an atmosphere composition report. They already had that, though, and knew it had been confirmed. What they were really after was his account of his time on the surface.

Eugene eased the conference room doors open and the men seated at the long table stood and began clapping. One by one they approached him, each muttering things like "Congratulations!" and "Job well done, son, well done indeed."

Once they were all seated, he found his place at a podium at the front of the room.

"Well," a man in a long coat said, "We have your reports. Good work, Dr. Silvagno. Really top-notch stuff. I know you've been through a lot. We all do. But I have to ask: what of the surface? We've got nothing on that. Well, not much, anyway. We're not questioning your motives—not at all, please understand that—but you have to tell us about it."

"Honestly," Eugene began, "I don't remember much. I know that sounds crazy, and you picked me because of my meteorological and geological expertise, but it's all a blur."

The men shifted uncomfortably and showered him with grave looks.

Dr. Silvagno sighed.

"Here's what I do remember. I touched down without a hitch. The ship stayed in orbit and the transport got away fine. I ran the composition programs, and everything checked out. You have to understand, I was ready to step outside no matter what."

"We have all reached that point," a man in one corner of the room bellowed in an irritated voice.

"Y—yes, I know," Eugene stammered, "But anyway, I did just that. I walked out. I took a deep breath. And I was fine."

They smiled elatedly at one another. A woman, red hair pinched into a tight bun on her scalp, motioned for him to continue.

"I started crying," he said. "Partially from joy, and partially from trying to get used to Alpha Centauri."

"Yes," the man in the long coat said, "Is it bearable? How would we fare?"

"It's fine. The radiation levels are nominal" Dr. Silvagno assured him. "It just takes some getting used to. It's all… I don't know," the doctor continued, "Spiritual. That's the only word I can use. A lot of it has to do with how impossibly blue the sky is. It's awkward at first. But, as I was saying, I started crying. When I finally pulled myself together and my eyes were adjusted, I started walking. There was vegetation everywhere. Not grass, like on Earth, but more of a teal, flat ivy that swept up and down the hill sides. There was a smell; a pungency about the place. It was quite spectacular. I extracted my camera and created several different sim-vids, which, I assume, all of you have been able to view."

They nodded quickly.

"Then something moved."

Gasps and mumbling erupted from Eugene's audience and they eyed him suspiciously.

"Why wasn't this in your report?" the man in the long coat asked in a low voice. "The Clonpulls recorded no evidence of life forms other than flora."

"It was naïve of you to assume there wouldn't be," Eugene said matter-of-factly.

That word, it seemed, continued to plague his subconscious.

They stared at him without blinking.

"For God's sake, it's almost an exact clone of Earth. What *did* you expect? That it would be sitting there, for billions of years, just waiting for *us* to come and populate it? That's not the way it works. That's not the way *life* works."

The man in the long coat stood and scowled at Dr. Silvagno.

"Don't lecture me, sir. If it wasn't for me, you would still be on Pangea fishing for new minerals to add to your catalogue—"

"That's enough!" the redhead shouted. She walked over to the man in the coat and asked him, in a polite, almost dainty voice, to be seated. Eugene couldn't help but smile at her.

"Please continue, Dr. Silvagno," she said.

The doctor ran his fingers through this hair.

"Well, like I said, something moved. Since I wasn't allowed to carry any weapons with me, I had to make a quick decision. I hadn't wandered too far from the transport; maybe fifty yards. But this animal, whatever it was, had locked on to me. I caught a glimpse of it moving in and out of an outcropping filled with large boulders. It kept low to the ground. My instinct was to run, but I didn't. I just stood there.

"It was then that I noticed the sounds of life all around me. There was a constant 'whir' at the site. Creatures with short, blunt limbs gathered at my feet. They looked like flattened frogs. I kicked at one—I'm not sure why I did that, but I did—and it immediately sprang into the air and darted off into the distance. Its body was one big wing, which flexed like an accordion in the middle—at the thorax—in order to achieve vertical lift. It utilized some sort of exoskeleton, as did most everything else I encountered. This likely accounts for the satellite discrepancy; the fact that the sensors can't penetrate the shell of the fiber cartilage."

To his amazement, the committee appeared bored. They weren't interested in his "Galapagos report"; they wanted facts about the habitability for humans. This infuriated Eugene, which further reinforced his desire to avoid telling them the story. In his childish logic, he decided they didn't care, so why should he? What he had discovered was, of course, of monumental importance, but he couldn't overcome the sensation to be blatantly stubborn.

Besides, he didn't want to be a teacher anymore. He had retired from that ages ago.

Despite the unexpected pang of selfishness that had taken hold, he knew "the doctor" residing within was on the verge of telling them the truth—something he had decided, three years into his return voyage, he would never do. And so far he hadn't been given a chance. Not twenty minutes after docking at the F.P.U. complex he had been whisked away, wrapped in clean, white plastic like a newborn baby, straight to the quarantine chamber for forty-eight hours of observation before being allowed to interact with the general populace.

Welcome home.

"And then," Silvagno continued, "It lunged at me. That's when I got a good look at it. It was something like a big spider... only not as coarse. You know, not covered in those sharp little filaments. There was the exoskeleton. And it moved much more fluidly. There were eight legs, which extended out to the sides. It was very fast—comparable to an antelope, perhaps."

He was lying. Though he did encounter such a being, it wasn't hostile in the least. In fact, it had approached him cautiously, like a cow at pasture, its row of nostrils flaring inquisitively, trying to identify his scent.

The truth was much more complicated.

Dr. Silvagno had remained on QR-491 for three days. When the planet turned away from Alpha Centauri on the first night, the whir around him ceased and the darkness was absolute. He fumbled around the landing site clumsily, his feet constantly tangling in the thickets of ivy.

Tired and frustrated, Eugene barked for the transport's computer to activate its lights. He hadn't realized that he was too far away for the computer to process his command.

The first sound he heard echoed through the brush, a long, drawn-out *clack* that caused him to start praying—an act, up until that point, that he had never done with any degree of sincerity.

Not even to Scuttlebug himself.

Chapter 5

The airlock snapped shut and Orion Esocrat was sealed inside his Korean issue home with two outlaws.

They removed their helmets and had sat at the table in his kitchen. Ori tried not to make eye contact with them.

He rummaged through his pantry, extracting various supplement containers, expecting to hear grumbling disapproval. After arranging the capsules neatly on a tray bearing the scars of serrated cutlery, he presented them to the women.

There, in the soft florescence buzzing overhead, he fully understood the magnitude of his dilemma.

Beanca was not Beanca. Beanca was Carla Grayson.

Orion had seen far too many Union documentaries on the history of the Graysons to not know who this brittle-looking intruder was. The smell of sweat wrung from hard labor wafted from the neck of her vacuusuit. Despite her overwhelming sense of desperation, the woman seemed remarkably carefree.

And now she sat here, in his hovel, with this mysterious traveler "Liza," gulping the oversized supplements with robotic efficienty, barely allowing themselves time to breathe.

"Thank you," Carla said after a time.

"Yeah," Liza added, "Grade-A, top-quality F.P.U. goods."

The panic on Orion's face was palpable. It was why he never even attempted to play poker.

"You know who I am," Carla said quietly. "Yes. You do. I don't care what you think of me. I really don't. I was under the impression that this was a place of refuge, for, you know, *us*."

She moved one hand slowly through the air, as if she were blessing the three of them.

"What 'us'?" he asked flatly.

"Worshipers of Scuttlebug," Carla said. "That's what you are, right? Isn't that what the people here do?"

She peered out the window and then glanced at Chiu. Pointing, she said, "I saw the temple when we landed. Don't try to act like it doesn't exist. I mean, you guys worship that worm thing—"

"Listen," Chiu cut in, "I don't see the point in keeping up this 'Liza' thing any longer. My name is Chiu. We just want to hide out here... just for a little while. We were under the impression Europa is good for that sort of thing."

The remainder of humanity had gone insane. Orion had come to that conclusion earlier in the temple. He thought it might be a rash conclusion, but, after listening to these two, who had likely killed Union Officials in order to steal a government ship, Ori was sure he was right.

These women were fools; for all their resourcefulness, they came to a colony sponsored solely by the Union. The F.P.U. kept logs, and the Officials that delivered their supplements knew faces. These fugitives wouldn't last more than two days.

"There was nowhere else for us to go," Carla urged. "This is it. Pluto is no picnic, Orion," she said, lowering her eyes.

"I know," he hissed. His unexpected malice silenced the room.

"I've served a rotation there. Before you were born. With your father."

Carla put one hand to her mouth and involuntarily began gnawing on her knuckles.

She sorely missed her father. He had died not long after her sixth birthday—executed, like the rest of her ancestors, just as soon as another member of the Grayson family had reached suitable working age.

That's when she noticed Orion's sim-vid, sitting idly against the back wall, its projection of 491 hovering at a reduced size.

"Do you like it here?" she asked.

Ori didn't know what to say. "No, not really," he thought, "but this is about as good as it gets. This *is* as good as it gets." Here Carla Grayson, more than likely the only person in the system who could trace back her ancestry in one direct line to Earth with certainty, was, it seemed, trying to have a genuine conversation with him.

"No," he said, "I don't. I hate it. But it's not possible to reach QR-491," he added, noting her interest in the sim-vid. "The F.P.U. hasn't completed the Borsen engine yet, so that's that. They'll find out you're here. They probably already know."

"Yes," she responded tiredly, "but we weren't going to stay here forever. In fact, we weren't going to stay here more than a few days. We're going to make it to the Headquarters at Neptune and hijack the Borsen transporter."

Orion, seeing no other feasible reaction, began laughing. "I'm not sure if you were listening to what I just said," he sputtered in between chortles, "but they haven't finished the engine yet. Even if they had, the security there is impenetrable. You would need more than a couple of vaccusuits and a makeshift weapon to get inside."

Carla and Chiu knew he was right. The former stood and began walking slowly around his home.

"In consideration of the many other places I could be," he finally said after a pause, "Europa is not that bad."

"Yes," she continued, "But it's still a miserable existence. Not as miserable as ours, you might say," she said to Chiu, "but miserable nonetheless. You have a large hovel here, Orion. Much larger than the other researchers, I noticed. That means you have some favor with the F.P.U. You, Mr. Esocrat, are an individual who's trusted."

He wouldn't fully admit it to himself, but, to a certain degree, she was right. For the most part, the Officials had always been kind to him (mainly because he was compliant and openly grateful for his post on one of the most civilized places in the solar system).

"That's why," she continued, "You're going to help us secure the transporter."

Carla quietly removed the chain gun from underneath her air pack. Orion hadn't even noticed it when they stood in the airlock for decompression. The thing had probably been fastened with little more than tape and chewed gum (if such luxuries—which he was sure were beyond the means of Carla Grayson—persisted).

Out of the nearest window he saw the congregation of Scuttlebug worshipers nearing his hovel, each carrying the obligatory confirmation gift of ice-sculpted

Scuttle larvae. This was awarded a new member upon acceptance, and it was placed, with great care, just outside the convert's primary airlock.

In essence, it was an intergalactic lawn gnome.

Several of the followers had crowded around the supply ship and were confusedly gesturing to one another. The women caught his glance and peered beyond the mob.

"If you tell any of them who we are, we'll take you outside and blow a hole in your plexifab."

His head trembled, but Orion managed to nod his assent. Carla hid the chain gun in a floor compartment, the bulk of its barrel barely lifting the cover. Ori rushed to the back of the room and returned with a dusty rug. He stretched it over the compartment, creating wrinkles in the fabric nearest the protrusion.

Chiu stood at the sound of the hissing airlock. The researchers gathered ten at a time in the entrance while the chamber pressurized. They clamored to look through the porthole, the first in line extending an elongated, oval chunk of Europan ice. "The Scuttlebug rebirth has found you!" they chanted eagerly. Pale sunlight filtered through the icy egg like stained glass, bathing the hovel in fractured Jovian twilight.

*   *   *

Dr. Silvagno exited the conference room with his head down and face averted as if he were a celebrity attempting to evade Paparazzi. Once he was in his room, he locked the door and settled into bed. He stared at the padded ceiling and waited, his knees rigid and knuckles clenched.

This was how it transpired.

There was a sharp jolt, and then the being from QR-491 seeped from his nostrils like a black fog.

Eugene had failed to truthfully finish the account of his experiences on the surface of the earth-like satellite, instead sputtering out some hopeful dribble about the Centurion planet and its endless supply of vegetation and, more importantly, air. That word, more than anything else, is what they longed for.

Air.

He knew that if he tossed it into his speech at just the right moment it would preoccupy them long enough for him to retreat down the narrow hall so he could recoil into the deepest recesses of his soul. This, he imagined, is the same place where the Gushkewau'—a name meaning "the darkness" that he had drawn from his studies of Native American linguistic records—now lived, and where it would reside until it decided the doctor had fully served his purpose.

Then it would inhabit others.

Eugene had come to the conclusion that Gushkewau' was capable of assuming control of humanity. As laughable as the idea appeared on the exterior, his gut told him it was true. Gushkewau' had emerged, just before dawn on the second day, as an opaque mist, cascading out from around the green eyeballs of a herd of pig-like creatures that grazed docilely near the landing site. They had held their heads low, gnawing dumbly on the ivy that stretched across the plains in every direction.

The darkness collected around them, and they didn't begin their high-pitched squealing until Gushkewau' had congealed. It looked like the mythical "ghost," moving in long, calculated strides, various parts of its anatomy still rising from clusters of the tortured animals. When it was over, they were all comatose. Their nerves allowed a mild protest in the form of mechanical twitching that was soon smoothed into a barely detectable quiver. They eventually succumbed to the gray flatness of death.

This had paralyzed Eugene. At first, Gushkewau' took no notice of him. It simply examined the fresh corpses; not like a hungry animal, but like a scientist, scrutinizing the bodies with care, seemingly trying to identify something (or, perhaps, *conclude* something).

After a short time it began to feed. The hindquarters of one dead creature, Eugene remembered, seemed to evaporate in the cloud.

It may have been the head of Gushkewau'. Maybe the whole thing was a head. It was alive, undoubtedly, and intelligent—but it didn't assume a stable form. Or, at the very least, it didn't appear to.

Dr. Silvagno had decided to make a run for it. It was the hastiest maneuver that he could've possibly executed, but cognitive thought was impossible.

His feet lighted through the tangled beds with surprising accuracy, and soon he saw his transport sitting idly in the distance. The doctor didn't think he would ever be happy to see that damned transport module, but he was. He actually wanted to return to the void and see *people*, those abominable creations, one more time.

The scientist in him knew he hadn't given this newly-discovered (and, by all accounts, unprecedented) creature a fair shake. Eugene had committed the cardinal sin of running instead of staying and observing.

His years of schooling had been promptly tossed out the proverbial window, and he was glad of it.

Something cold had penetrated him, and instinct took over. It was time to go.

When he was within fifty feet, Eugene shouted to the computer to ignite the thrusters. The bulky piece of machinery illuminated, and a white curl of exhaust rolled out from underneath.

That's when he realized he'd been absorbed.

Dr. Silvagno fell to the ground slowly. He couldn't think. His brain tried to tell him that he had stepped out into space. He prepared for the bitter taste of blood and the constricting of arteries that he knew would follow.

But none of that happened. Instead, he arose, in a daze, his arms outstretched and hands limp before him like a zombie. Eugene flexed his fingers absently and stared past them at the transport. It idled loudly, ready for take-off.

He entered the hatch and began entering coordinates into the computer's nav-system. The herd of dead pigs was quickly lost among the widening plain of ivy.

Now, all these years later, this Gushkewau' hovered over Dr. Silvagno in the F.P.U. Headquarters. Its dark mass explored the room quietly, Eugene's personal effects and trinkets disappearing into the haze as it went.

In his mind Eugene was standing barefoot on a beach, which had been perfectly reconstructed (right down to the abandoned Goodyear tire bobbing in the surf) from an original historical sim-vid that he had paid an obscene amount of money for.

The water was cold on his feet. He enjoyed the way they sank into the murk with the ebbing tide; so much so, in fact, that he wasn't paying any attention to the figure that had approached him.

It was his father—but it wasn't. His eyes were different. If there was one thing he remembered about his father, it was his eyes. They were alert, sharp—full of life. These eyes were gray and unfocused. The entity smiled at him.

"Hello, Eugene," it said.

"You're not my father," Dr. Silvagno replied.

"You're very astute," the man replied. "No, I'm not. I'm Gushkewau', as you have chosen to call me. It's a curious name, don't you think?"

"What are you doing to me?"

"I'm studying you. And, if you really want to know the whole truth of it, I'm slowly eating you."

"What do you want to know about me? Just kill me now. Let's get it over with."

Gushkewau' released a sound that resembled laughter and probed an overturned crab with a piece of driftwood, its legs flexing rhythmically as it tried to right itself.

"No," it replied. "Your language is unlike any other I've encountered. It's so vocal."

Gushkewau' grinned and stood, placing a hand on Eugene's shoulder.

"Why are you doing this?" Eugene asked quietly, the panic in his voice rising. "I know, over those four years, there was a purpose to the nightmares. There was a reason for it all."

"Yes," Gushkewau' said, "There was and still is. The reason, Eugene, is that I had to learn how to communicate with you. We're symbiotic now." Dr. Silvagno's father turned toward his son. "Do you understand? Yes, you do. You're an educated man." At this he chuckled again. "You knew I was with you all along, Dr. Silvagno. We couldn't talk, I mean *really talk*, until we were back. Just imagine, if we had been carrying on like this for four years, those men you just talked with would think you were cracked. And then you'd be no good to anyone. So it was better to learn and pool. Then I'd be ready. Then you'd be ready."

Gushkewau' strolled down the beach and reached the tire just as it became wedged into a pile of crushed shells. He stuck one foot in the center and began dragging it along the shoreline.

"I still don't know what you are," Eugene said. "All I know is cold. That's all I've learned from you."

Gushkewau' reached Dr. Silvagno and took a seat on the tire. "I'm not as complicated as all that," he said. "I just want to learn. That's all I've ever wanted to do, even in my own system, which, by the way, is not "QR-491". I'm an example of curiosity; I'm an example," the creature said softly, "of that saying—you know the one. 'Curiosity killed the cat.' It's something like that. Only they couldn't kill this cat."

He laughed again.

"So here I am with you, now. There's something about you and your kind, Eugene. Even at your primitive stage of development, you managed to survive the death of your star and perpetuate your species. I feel there is much more for me to understand about 'humanity,'" Gushkewau' concluded coldly.

"I intend to consume until I reach my fill."

It then wandered down the beach, startling gulls as it went.

Chapter 6

Carla moved to the crumpled rug and removed the chain gun from its compartment in the floor, throwing the slender weapon over one shoulder and gesturing for Chiu to move away from Orion.

"Okay," she said gruffly, "We're getting out of here. Mr. Esocrat, you've got ten minutes to pack your essentials."

Orion glanced nervously around his living room. He had to take the Schultz converter: that was a no-brainer. Beyond that, he wasn't sure.

In every other Expansion Event that had occurred since he was eleven, he had never had any trouble throwing his valuables into a sack and digging deeper into outer system space. For the first time, though, he found that his thoughts were muddled.

He hastily jerked several jumpsuits from the closet and stuffed them in his bag, and was soon in the process of salvaging his favorite sim-vids from the console when Carla jabbed the barrel of her gun into his lower ribs.

"We have to go," she said with stout resolve. "Put on your vaccusuit."

Orion did as he was told. There wasn't any time to think it through. Before he knew it they were all crammed in the airlock as the mechanisms whirred, waiting for exposure. The decompression was slow and deliberate. Carla powered on the chain gun and a high, electric sizzle squealed and subsequently vanished with the escaping air.

"What are you doing?" Orion asked anxiously. "I'm not going to run."

It was true. He was too weak for that, and he had become resigned to the idea of being bullied into raiding the F.P.U. Headquarters.

In some completely insane way, it seemed inevitable; logical.

"It's not for you," she said in a hushed voice. The door slid open and he understood. Researchers were clamoring around the commandeered ship in droves. It seemed to Ori that they *pulsed*, and the notion hit him—as blasphemous as it was— that they had discovered something new to worship.

In reality, the congregation was trying to interpret what it was that the great and powerful Scuttlebug was telling them about their future. They were trying desperately to make sense of this unexplained breach in protocol.

Tryson was the first to see the trio exit the hovel. He rushed over and began relentlessly firing questions.

"Why would an F.P.U. Official allow this vessel to be docked here? Why would you do this to us? Look at the others. This act has shaken the very foundations of their faith—"

A researcher interrupted their conversation, plowing through them dumbly, sprinting across the ice toward a home that sat nestled against the slope of a frozen crag near the temple.

As much as Ori hated to admit it, Tryson was right. The moon was in an uproar.

It was then that Orion fully understood the magnitude of their mental instability.

Insanity here, in this place, was incurable. Once it had infected a person, it existed in some sort of plasma state, osmosing into the soul and rooting itself there, unmovable, like the fabled redwoods he had marveled at in the sim-vids passed down to him from his grandfather.

Like the titanic trees, it blots out everything else, as if it were a ghastly umbrella.

Orion had seen it claim many before him, and he wasn't sure how he had been able to avoid it.

But that didn't matter. He was about to leave both Europa and the Beast; the only two things that had really ever given him a run for his money.

The look on Tryson's face shifted into disbelief.

It was Carla. Her visor wasn't tinted, and the priest had recognized her infamous features.

His eyes were pale and wide, his mouth partially open.

Suddenly, the holy man raised both bulbous hands and shouted, "My brothers! Here, among us now, we have the physical embodiment of Scuttlebug's most dangerous enemy!"

Silence washed over the hysterical congregation. They all turned to their leader.

The Beast swirled in the moment of jarring quiet.

"We have in our midst the one and only—*the* Carla Grayson."

Ghostly whispers filled the bobbing helmets.

"It's all too clear," he continued, "That she has come to end our work. She has come to orchestrate the destruction of Scuttlebug and His followers. She has come to prevent our salvation."

At this the hushed banter evolved into a stark, unified roar. The mob surged forward, intent on murdering the intruder.

Orion backpedaled until he was cornered against the ship. Carla appeared at his side, chain gun exposed, the magazine primed. Chiu looked over her shoulder and, seeing what was coming, quickly joined them against the hull.

"Don't..." Tryson snarled. "Scuttlebug doesn't forgive you for murder. Not like this."

"Brother," he continued in an attempt to appeal to the recent convert, "Have we not accepted you? Are you not one of our own? You too will experience the salvation that only Scuttle can deliver, but you must—"

Chiu snatched the chain gun from Carla's shoulder and squeezed the aluminum trigger.

Tryson was hit first. A gurgle resounded in every ear-link, and red flecked the curvature of his visor. The next rounds tore through the closest researchers, each ones' vaccusuit rhythmically spewing blue-gray snake streams of O2. The fabric where the rounds had entered glowed an iridescent orange that simmered and was just as quickly snuffed out by the everlasting cold.

Sanders, a researcher whose hovel was not far from Orion's, had broken off from the crowd and worked his way quietly around the arc of the ship's thrusters. He scaled the repair ladder on the port side and secured his footing in preparation for his barbarous descent onto the heretics.

Chiu looked up just as he connected.

Sanders' feet dealt Carla a concussion, leaving her sprawled in a ragged "T" against the landing gear. The seemingly rabid researcher was up again before either Orion or Chiu had realized they'd been attacked. The wheezing madman wrapped up Chiu from behind.

In desperation, the fugitive fired the chain gun wildly, only just missing Ori as he lifted Carla over his shoulder and deposited her into the supply ship's now gaping hatch.

The surface underneath them began to melt into shallow pools under the heat of the burrowing ammunition. Orion had scaled the ladder and strapped Carla into the co-pilot's chair when he noticed a contingency of researchers approaching, at full sprint, from the collection of hovels on the horizon.

"The scuttlebugs!" they shouted, "They're moving!"

A grave slab of comprehension settled on Orion, and he felt like an idiot for not realizing it before.

The heat.

Just as they congregated around thermal pockets on the seabed, they were attracted to the smoldering rounds now cooking the long frigid surface.

Reprogramming the ship's sim-vid, he patched its connection into his suit's computer. The CPU began to monitor the heaving mammals beneath the ice.

At first they were little more than sluggish holographic blips. But then, with stunning speed, they began vanishing and reappearing in erratic patterns. They looked like static.

It was the teleportation.

"A nest has been penetrated," one of the researchers reported softly. "A mother has been killed."

Without any sound, as was the custom of the blunt physics that applied to this airless prison they inhabited, the surface began to tremble.

It was barely noticeable at first. After every breath Orion felt the animals' protests in his joints. Eventually it became an audible rattle as his suit's components gave way.

Soon it was the pulse of Europa. "This place," Orion thought numbly, "*is* alive."

Enormous, translucent shadows materialized just beneath the researchers' feet. Sanders had given up on securing either Chiu or the chain gun. Along with the others, he moved at a brisk pace toward the temple, chanting incantations as he went.

The pulse evolved; became a throb.

Orion pulled himself up the ladder and cautiously motioned to his cohort, who dropped the gun and was on his heels in an instant. Once Chiu was in, he ordered the computer to seal the hatch. Ori punched in the code for the vessel's nav-system to engage the autopilot—to follow its default course to the Headquarters at Neptune.

At first, Ori wasn't sure if the engines had fired. There was tremendous shaking, then the shriek of tired metal.

For reasons he couldn't explain, he briefly speculated this was what the shifting of tectonic plates had been like.

Suddenly, the vessel leaned to one side and began to rock steadily like an infant determined to complete her first full tumble.

Then it was careening through the ether. Plastered to their seats, the fugitives could do little more than close their eyes and focus on keeping lunch from making an unwelcome reappearance.

The boosters relaxed, and Orion managed to slow his breathing and eventually peer out of the starboard window.

Ori saw something inexplicable; in the spot their vessel occupied only moments earlier a Union freighter fired its thrusters and settled into the chaos unfolding on the surface. The ungainly craft slowly carved its nose through the melting sheet like an interstellar anteater.

He couldn't make any sense of it.

Then the primordial ice gave way as if it were an ancient caldera.

Initially, he could only surmise that this mystery ship had received a tip as to the whereabouts of the escaped convicts. They were probably mercenaries working for a hefty fee; a permanent residence at Headquarters, perhaps.

"They must've seen this happening over the playback monitors," he finally murmured. Turning to his fellow travelers, he said, "They must think you're still down there."

Carla remained unconscious, but Chiu watched as a single Official, now a particle of a man, emerged and scurried across the collapsing expanse.

Chiu removed Carla's helmet and began running her vitals through the computer. Orion moved to the surveillance monitors hissing on the bridge. In grainy detail, he watched the research station complete its descent into the frozen hell that lay beneath. The adjacent monitor showed the Temple as it split in two, right down the seams of the giant Scuttlebug idol. It was soon a pile of rubble, and, to Orion's amazement, several of the never-before-seen creatures clattered onto the foundation of the church in brilliant flashes.

Like inchworms, they hulked, as best they could, toward the destroyed sanctuary.

Many died within seconds of interstellar exposure, the downward curve of their mammoth tusks trying futilely to tunnel through the almost impenetrable surface. Some, it seemed, were able to teleport back to safety.

The Official that had escaped ran toward the ruins of the temple.

"All those years of gathering data," Orion muttered under his breath. "Gone."

Three animals had died in the struggle to protect their nest; they looked like beached whales.

As the ship rocketed up toward the rocky belt at the edge of Jupiter, Orion wondered if the Beast had witnessed the event in its entirety. He wondered, too, if it was the first time these creatures had made it to the surface. It was certainly the first time any of them had traversed the frostbitten confines of the once mighty cathedral.

Chapter 7

They wanted Dr. Silvagno to be on hand for the first official test of the Borsen transporter. Even though they were more than a little disgruntled at his abrupt departure from the board meeting, the consensus was that he had done more than enough to earn a seat at the demonstration.

Accompanied by two couriers in black robes, he walked hurriedly down the narrow corridors of the F.P.U. complex.

Upon entering the viewing room, light applause broke out once again.

Eugene blushed. He despised being the center of attention. The doctor nodded absently, having devoted all mental energies to imagining the way the rest of history would play itself out if the transporter were successful.

Likely, mankind would saturate QR-941 like a virus, and, within another millennium, deplete it of all natural resources. Then, he speculated, a new and improved Pynchon orbiter would be developed.

"No," he thought grimly, "they would all say that it was 'completely safe'." After all, Alpha Centauri is millions of times larger than the Sun.

It couldn't possibly happen again.

Dr. Silvagno slid into his chair at the fringe of the plush conference room. Neptune beckoned just outside the pentagonal window.

"Gentlemen," the familiar redhead said loudly, "It is time. What you are about to see is the future—this transporter will save our species, something that our fathers and forefathers had dreamed of for centuries; an existence without threat of Expansion."

She carried on in this fashion for some time, her hands continuously pointing to the window and moving excitedly. All Eugene could think about was the futility of it all.

All the while, the entity was continually pressing at the base of his skull.

He had hoped to find some way to exorcise the demon when he returned to Neptune, but, a year into his return journey, he had realized it was hopeless. In fact, it seemed a real possibility that the only way he could be definitively purged would be in the event of his death. The sincerity with which it stated its intention to prey upon his gray matter meant only one thing; it would satisfy its voracious appetite. It would likely chew through a vital portion of his brain stem, and then it would have no choice but to move on. Of course, it would then be too late for the doctor.

Despite the bleak scenario, he hadn't completely abandoned the notion that there had to be a way to flush out the creature without extinguishing his own life. Until he had a definitive method for purging the beast, it was best kept secret. A selfish notion, for sure, but one that might ultimately save him *and* what was left of humanity.

Eugene's gut told him that the exact opposite was likely to come to fruition.

"Now," the redheaded Official interjected curtly, "The test begins."

Clapping fluttered through the room when the lights dimmed. Though only barely engaged, Eugene had managed to hear her say that the transporter, though currently too far away to see, would conduct its test at the outskirts of the Adams ring system.

Everyone stared at the curvature of the mammoth debris pattern in stolid anticipation. For what seemed an eternity, the hazy line of asteroids and chunks of billion year-old ice disappeared at the apex on the far side of the planet.

Then a brilliant flash erupted, and, just as quickly, was squelched into darkness.

Dr. Silvagno posited it a supernova on a comprehendible scale.

"Ladies and gentlemen," the emcee continued, "You have just witnessed the revolution of space travel. The Borsen transporter has made the journey to Pluto and back in the very instant you witnessed the ignition spark; less than 0.259 milliseconds."

The board members were ecstatic. A rarity grabbed everyone's attention, including Dr. Silvagno's, as a champagne cork whizzed past his head and collided flatly against the padded back wall. The frothy liquid overflowed onto the floor, and one of the couriers in black entered carrying crystal glasses that glinted on trays. He smiled and nodded to the Officials courteously, presenting them with, in the other hand, a pewter dish covered in piping morsels.

Food. *Real* food.

"My God," Eugene said to no one in particular, "It's been ten years since I've seen—or smelled—the *real deal*."

Small bits of chicken steamed, the plastic toothpicks at their centers erect, waiting to be plucked. Bread, no doubt bitter and made edible by the addition of globs of synthetic butter, was stacked in rows neatly alongside some type of broiled pork.

"Supplements," he said bitterly, "We've all been choking down supplements for God knows how long." The doctor breathed deeply. "Because 'there is no more food.'"

He stood on the verge of releasing an angry protest when the sound of shattering glass diverted him. The boisterous chatter dissolved into unsettling silence.

Slowly, each head turned toward the viewing window.

Hundreds of thousands of miles away, a thin trail of debris diverged from the steady path of Adams. It tapered off in a peppermint swirl, vanishing into...nothing.

No stars, no light, no reflection of the deep blue below. It was a conspicuous absence against the backdrop of a billion brilliant stars.

Eugene understood at once, and his heart thrummed sickly.

A black hole.

The vast majority of onlookers were bewildered, trying desperately to rationalize this freak occurrence.

Apparently the redhead had understood too. She glanced nervously around the room, seeing if anyone else had been able to comprehend the situation. Her eyes locked with Eugene's.

The woman tore herself away from his gaze and began addressing each official by first name. Her gait suddenly serious, she moved quickly around the room, discussing the occurrence with everyone in abrasive half-whispers. Several declared her a liar. Undaunted, she asked them all to relocate to their quarters until the proper research could be conducted and a more "suitable" explanation produced.

They were less than satisfied. Filing out of the room irritably, they cursed and a balding fellow with yellow teeth spat.

The redhead collapsed into an empty seat near the window.

"I don't think we've been properly introduced. I'm Eugene. Eugene Silvagno."

"Isn't it 'Doctor'?" the woman asked sarcastically.

"Yes," he responded in his most matter-of-fact tone. "But you can call me Eugene."

"Great. I'm Sonja Lewin. And we're all about to die."

They didn't shake hands. Eugene settled into the chair next to hers and peered through the Coke-bottle thickness of the oversized porthole.

The debris trail had thickened.

Part of him couldn't help wondering if the food strewn across the floor was still warm.

*   *   *

Orion sat facing Carla. Chiu was working quietly in a corner, checking the weapons lining the rack, slapping magazines into the butts of guns mechanically.

He moved close to the unconscious felon and brushed the strands of silver away from her face. With her helmet now removed and her head motionless, he studied her features; he began to understand why so many people had billed her as "ugly."

Her nose hadn't been produced in a mold like so many of the Union women Ori had encountered. It was natural, and bore its flaws without shame. There was a small bump at the bridge; perhaps it had been broken at one time and improperly set. Her chin was narrow and flat.

Orion smiled at her. As contrary as it ran to the universal consensus, he found her utterly mesmerizing.

Carla's eyelids fluttered. She sat up and recognized Orion in front of her. He was still smiling. Reflexively, she smiled back.

"Thank you," she said. Orion stared, his smile now crooked with surprise.

"For what?"

"For saving my life. No one—well, no one outside of the prison colonies, anyway—has ever done anything like that for me."

He wasn't even sure why he had done it. He could've very well left her to face the wrath of the seething alien horde, but, for whatever reason, he had decided that was unacceptable. The more he thought about his split-second decision, the more he conjectured the likely consequences.

If he had left both her and Chiu on Europa, he could've returned the Union supply ship to Neptune himself and been hailed a hero. Perhaps he could've negotiated some sort of deal where he could live out the rest of his life aboard Headquarters. At least that would have been somewhat humane. At least he would have enjoyed the company of the mentally sound.

"Anyhow," she began again, reading his face, "I might not be worth all that effort. I mean, you'll probably be relocated to a comet or something."

It was true: he would likely be made an example.

A comet, though? Unlikely.

The F.P.U. didn't kill unless it was absolutely necessary, and being dropped off on Hale-Bopp amid a blizzard of radiation, with a vacant sense of duty as only the most heinous offenders had experienced, was impossible. He could argue his case.

After all, it was Chiu that had fired the chain gun and provoked the scuttlebugs. He

was only trying to save his life and the lives of those nearest to him. He was only

trying to preserve the human race.

"I killed a man," she said abruptly. Orion looked at her cautiously. He could

tell she wasn't lying.

"But he didn't really leave me a choice," she added defensively. "It was him,

or us. I gave him the option of leaving the ship. We were still close enough to Pluto—

he could've jettisoned down. It would've worked. He could've stayed in the

dormitory until help arrived."

Carla unexpectedly burst into tears.

"But he wouldn't move," she sobbed.

Chiu left the weapons rack and stood behind her, both hands on her friend's

shoulders.

Orion felt genuine sorrow for Carla. For the first time, he understood that she

was, in fact, entirely human. He was unsure how that fact had eluded him.

Still, he had to admit that she possessed an intangible "otherwordly" quality.

To have survived the physical and mental torment that she and her ancestors

had endured for so many centuries, and to still feel guilt about something as

relatively mundane as icing an Official who threatened death—he realized he would

not have been so righteous.

It made her that much more attractive.

Over the course of the next hour, the steady rumble of the engines lulled the crew into tranquility. Orion thought about saying something, but it would have only been for the sake of pleasantries.

And they were all so tired.

The panels flashed and immersed the interior of the ship in varying tones of emerald.

Ori was exhausted, but he didn't want to sleep. He stood and moved to the minuscule porthole.

Jupiter was now a cloudy dot, barely visible in a sea of stars.

Inexplicably, this sated his sense of apprehension. Ori eased his aching shoulders against the wall and allowed the artificial gravity to do its work. The diamond pattern engrained in the metal massaged his lumbar in the slow descent.

Unable to resist the urge any longer, he closed his eyes and slept.

*   *   *

The alarm. Carla and Chiu were at the helm, punching commands into the panel, trying desperately to alter their trajectory. Numbed by sleep, Orion stood on wobbly legs, gathering what strength remained in order to pull himself up to eye-level with the porthole.

"Proximity alert," the nav-system repeated calmly. "An unknown object is within one mile of the hull."

It was a ship; a large ship.

It blotted out the stars.

The ship grew larger still, and Ori saw that it wasn't a Union freighter as he had feared. There were strange markings along the length of the bow. For all intents and purposes, they were unintelligible.

"Orion!" Carla shouted. "If you know anything about these ships, you better get over here and take over. Now." Moved by a spike of adrenaline, he darted to the controls.

"Wh—what," he stammered, "What the hell is going on?"

"It's a salvage vessel," Chiu said, "They're commandeering our ship for parts."

"They're commandeering an F.P.U. ship? Are they insane?"

Carla pointed to the sim-vid. A three-dimensional display of all three of them sprang from the monitor. An urgent bulletin read:

Three fugitives—two escaped from Pluto. The third, a researcher who has abandoned his post, and is hereby convicted of aiding and abetting. They have stolen a federal ship, ID#: FPU-998402. Reward: $4,000,000 and a Headquarters flat to whoever returns them—**alive**—to Central Complex.

Their images rotated slowly, periodically magnifying their faces in order to provide a more accurate description. "Christ," Orion said under his breath, "We've got to do something."

"What, exactly? They've latched onto us. We're not going anywhere."

Ori scrambled back up to the porthole and saw that it was true. Four cables were taut and had already begun to reel them in.

He dropped down, mired in thought. If they fired their boosters at full power, it would tear the ship apart. The cables, he postulated, were polycomposite. They wouldn't give. It was best to power down.

"Turn off the engines," he said quietly, "We need to conserve fuel."

"What?" Carla asked sullenly. "*Turn off the engines*? Are you out of crazy?"

"They've latched on," he said. "It's no use."

"Maybe we can drag them to—"

"We can't," Orion broke in. "It won't work. Their ship is three times bigger than ours. Turn them off, now. It's the only way to keep the reactor fully charged. It might be enough for us to break away if we get the chance."

Chiu mumbled obscenities, but did as she was told. The three of them stood, without speaking, for some time. Outside the ship, they heard the whine of intrusive docking gear. Orion unlocked the hatch. Neither Carla nor Chiu argued the point.

Through the rectangular pane of plexifab, he saw the entrance of the other ship slide open. There was only darkness. He backed away when he finally saw eyes, several pairs of them, glowing reflective in the dull light produced by the control panel behind him.

Ori was sure they belonged to wolves.

Chapter 8

Initially, Dr. Silvagno thought his arrival had been a dream; that he was still light-years from his destination, and that he'd only just crested the parabolic arc that sent him on the "downward curve" of his unfathomably long journey.

But then there were the intermittent pinpricks of light; the tell-tale flecking of cosmic radiation that flooded his vision with erratic fireworks that, he thought, were startlingly reminiscent of synapses.

As R.E.M. set in, the doctor was unnaturally forced into a more keen level of consciousness. He knew he was caught in the throes of deep slumber, yet he was somehow able to manipulate the world around him and—for lack of a better word—"control" his actions.

Then the creature appeared, and an impressionist landscape unfolded in dramatic swathes.

The sky was a cold magenta, as if stuck in perpetual twilight. Meteorites raked the atmosphere. The surface, coated in a substance he imagined to be crystallized methane, quavered.

Gushkewau', now inhabiting the likeness of none other than Albert Einstein, placed the ever-familiar tire in the goo and took a seat next to Eugene.

"I'd prefer it if we no longer had these encounters," the despondent physicist muttered. "If you're going to kill me, then get on with it."

"No. Not yet. Soon, but there is still work to be done. That 'black hole' out there, currently devouring what's left of your system: you're going to enter it."

"What?"

"You heard me. You're going to breach the event horizon and be *consumed*."

So this was it. The thing had had enough of haunting the corners of this universe and was ready to throw in the towel. All the better. Hell, maybe he would jettison himself from an airlock just before reaching the anomaly so the organism would suffer all the more.

Gushkewau' processed the doctor's thoughts, shook his head, and knowingly twirled one end of his push-broom mustache.

"That won't kill me. If you do that, you'll die, and I'll simply be confined to temporary boredom. Eventually I'll make my way to the 'Headquarters,' and then I'll absorb everyone. In fact, I'll make sure they know it was you who was responsible for the extinction of your species. How does that sound?"

Dr. Silvagno didn't believe him. When he was on QR-491, this creature had attacked a herd of extremely primitive animals. He also knew why the creature inhabited the planet in the first place. It was stuck.

Eugene didn't know how or why, but, by some power the doctor couldn't comprehend, the phantasm had been forced to inhabit the distant world. If it was no problem for it to leave and learn about intelligent races such as his own, as Gushkewau' seemed hell-bent on doing, why would it spend time probing a dull herd of intergalactic omnivores?

It saw Dr. Silvagno's thoughts. The wild-haired apparition frowned and chewed on a pipe he had drawn from the breast of his corduroy jacket. Eugene thought he had finally called its bluff.

"If you really mean to do that," the being declared in faux-Germanic tones, "It will result only in your death—and, though brief, a decidedly excruciating one, I might add. Have no illusions, Dr. Silvagno. I am greater than the trifles of non-atmospheric space."

Eugene didn't respond. Gushkewau' stood and brushed off his trousers, which were unevenly crosshatched with the pale remnants of careless chalk handling. He looked out over the viscous pudding and smiled.

"How do you think I came to be in your galaxy in the first place? The thing you call a 'black hole' is a gateway. As a scientist, I would imagine that you'd have some curiosity about it."

It was true; he was excited by the potential power of black holes. He didn't know whether or not to believe this entity. All of the research and formulas that he had studied concerning singularities indicated that no solid object—much less an organic being—could survive entry and assimilation. Honestly, what chance would he have if even photons were doomed?

And why would this thing tell him to do something that would almost certainly destroy them both? Was it because he knew Eugene well enough to know that if he instructed him to enter the black hole, he would spend absurd amounts of time considering why it had told him to do this and therefore conclude that it really *did not* want him to cross the threshold? Had Gushkewau' realized, through his intricate knowledge and expertise of the way Eugene's mind reasons and postulates that he would eventually understand that entering the black hole is the only true way to kill it once and for all?

The doctor found himself trying to quantify what he knew about the creature's existence. As he had time and again, Eugene found that there was really only one conclusion that could be drawn: he knew nothing. Resistance was futile. Eugene's intellect was far inferior to that of the amorphous monster, and that's all there was to it.

Still, like the white dwarf, the man found himself clinging to a vain sliver of hope.

Gushkewau' had told him that it could effortlessly move from any physical being to another, but what if there were essentials that it wasn't telling him (as there almost certainly were)? What if it had to remain in a body for a certain length of time in order to gather enough nutrients to prolong its life? Surely it had restrictions. After all, it too was living—it wasn't ethereal. It wasn't God.

If it were, why did it bother with questions that it already knew the answers to?

As the mathematician vanished amid the mist, Dr. Silvagno knew, in the pit of his stomach, that there was only one outcome.

For better or worse, he would, despite a myriad of attempts to muster a feasible alternative, traverse the plane where space and time unravel.

What some of his colleagues had labeled "a puncture in existence."

*   *   *

Orion backed away from the hatch as it completed its pressurization process. Once it slid open, the iridescent eyes stopped moving and remained fixed in the blackness. They looked like fireflies at the border of something wild.

Ori perceived indecipherable guttural utterances coming from the obscurity that lay ahead. Slowly, one of their captors emerged from the darkness and stood, slightly hunched, before them.

It was humanoid; that much was clear. The short, stocky build and elongated facial features were odd, but it was, in fact, distinctly human. The creature stood before them, covered in a thin layer of coarse dark hair, the plump digits of its right "hand" drumming thoughtfully against its chin.

"I am addressed as Fralin," it said in a raspy voice (and, much to the fugitives' surprise, startlingly clear English). "You are the ones who have stolen the Union supply ship."

So *it* was actually *he*. The first thought that ran through Orion's mind was gene manipulation. It was a common practice among AWOL researchers (especially those from Io). The consensus was that they were barely able to scrape by, circumventing the most remote parts of the solar system, mining their resources from dislodged Kuiper objects.

"I can see you've never encountered any of our kind before," Fralin said. "It always seems to be quite the shock. The language, too, is difficult. It's Roverian—a language that many of us feel is more natural than what the ancients spoke." He smiled, revealing a stained row of uneven canines.

"Well, since you'll be with us for quite a while, I suppose we should get the preliminaries out of the way."

Fralin began pacing the bridge of the captured ship restlessly, both arms behind his back like a general surveying troops before battle.

"We don't particularly care for the F.P.U., no matter what you might think. What we do care for, however, is money. And this ship—and its cargo—are worth a substantial amount." He inspected the control panel, carefully shielding his eyes from direct contact with the bulbs.

Another member of this exotic species then stepped aboard the ship—a female, Orion guessed—her features slightly more gracile than that of this alpha male.

She didn't introduce herself. Quietly, the female slipped into a position behind Carla and Chiu, waiting patiently for Fralin to complete his inspection.

"We're hybrids, of sorts," he finally said to Orion. "Our ancestors found it necessary to adapt as quickly as possible—to retain as much body heat as we could." He moved away from the panel and motioned for them to enter the gaping doorway. Carla glanced briefly at her companions.

Fralin, a muffled snarl curling his upper lip, read their eyes.

"Don't be foolish. We won't get paid if we harm you, but that doesn't mean we won't make things unpleasant. We are going to return this vessel, collect our reward, and that's all there is to it," he said absently. Motioning to the foreign entryway, he asked, as might a courtier, "Shall we?"

The trio left the supply ship without protest. Several other hybrids—some whose gender Ori found to be indistinct—appeared at their rear toting what looked like modified stunners. They were almost certainly lethal.

Instinctively, Orion held Carla's hand and felt his way along the corridor blindly. It was pitch and wholly unsettling. He had traversed the inky corners of this galactic highway just as often as anyone else, but even then there was artificial luminescence. Here, the sense that one was being swallowed pervaded everything.

Ori felt several of the hybrids brush past him in the opposite direction, the steel wool of their coats scraping noisily against his clothing. Upon turning around, he was barely able to glimpse (with the aid of the now diminishing light emanating from the nav-system control panel) the dim silhouettes of the hybrids as they began the process of securing the supply ship—likely removing otherwise unaffordable parts that they could claim as "stolen" by the criminal entourage. The familiar hatch finally snapped shut, and there were only the sounds of padded footsteps.

The hybrids smelled awful. Orion found himself making a subconscious effort to breathe through his mouth. The stench became more pungent the deeper they moved into the heart of the vessel. It was a wild, undomesticated fragrance.

In all likelihood, it was more natural than anything else he had ever smelled. It was, in his estimation, utterly unmasked. Ori imagined it was what QR-491 smelled like: a complete absence of synthetics.

The shuffling stopped. An amber lamp was ignited and they saw that they were in a room full of cages. Animals—real, live animals—of various species moved stealthily in their enclosures.

"This," Fralin said, pointing to the cage nearest them, "Is a wolf."

It growled and chewed at the cage door.

"Our genetic composition contains select parts of wolf, because, from the data we've gathered, they were the most acclimated of the animals we have been able to obtain."

He spoke like a tenured professor.

"Notice the heavy follicles covering the entire body. This sequence of DNA has provided us with a greatly increased amount of warmth over the centuries. Space can be unforgiving when heat coils are damaged. We were never welcome in the ports," he mused bitterly, "Because of our forefathers' decisions. They believed—"

"I don't care," Orion cut him off. "What the hell does all of this have to do with us?"

Fralin appeared profoundly offended. His forehead, with its low brow line and emphatic slope, gathered in wrinkles as he moved away from the researcher.

"As I was saying," he continued hoarsely, "Particular sequences have provided us with advantages that Homo sapiens consider... well... 'freakish'."

He chuckled, to no one in particular, and pointed a clawed index finger at one of his fiery eyes.

"We can see infinitely better in an absence of light than you'll ever be able to; another gift from our friend the wolf."

The wolf had backed into a corner of the cage, apparently resigned to its inability to mangle this new threat.

Moving through the room, they encountered several more cages, all filled with animals that were thought (or, at least, had been advertised as) extinct centuries prior to the Expansion. A chimpanzee squealed as they approached, its wiry arms jerking at bars angrily.

"We have blended small parts of this primate's genetics with our own," the hybrid continued. "Although many of my comrades have considered this a regression in our own evolution, there are extinct advantages to possessing tensile abilities."

He removed one boot, and they saw that his feet were, like the chimp's, made for grasping. And, directing everyone's attention overhead, they saw in the low light an intricate series of cables. Orion had noticed them briefly when entering the ship, but, as everyone else, he simply assumed they were power and nav-system hardware. Now, upon further inspection, it was clear that they composed a complex network. Further ahead of them in the darkness a series of low grunts were heard echoing down a hall. Two hybrids swung steadily by overhead, traveling with impressive speed.

"Where did you get all of these animals?" Orion asked. "I've never heard of anyone seeing any of these alive. They've been extinct since the migration."

Fralin nodded.

"That's what you've been told, friend. In fact, there are mercenaries and dealers that have managed to breed these animals. Like us, they don't like conducting business with the F.P.U. Sometimes, though, it is necessary."

After a period of silence, Carla spoke up. For the first time, Ori heard her voice tremble.

"What will you do with us?"

Fralin moved away from Orion and hobbled over to Carla and Chiu, sporadically placing his weight on padded knuckles as he went. The pair stood away from Orion and the rest of the hybrids.

"We will turn you over to the Union. You seem harmless enough, unlike many of the fugitives we intercept, but $4,000,000 is $4,000,000. And we have been drifting for a long, long time. Supplements have become grating."

"We're all tired of supplements," Orion broke in angrily. "Maybe you've been in the void a little *too* long. We're not from Headquarters, backed by the full and unwavering support of the F.P.U."

"I know what kind of lives you live," Fralin said mutely. "The lives of slaves. And I can tell by the look on your face that you are slowly realizing that you were always destined for servitude. You've come to terms with this recently, I assume." His eyes shone.

"I know this because you're angry. Most Union associates are hollow and defined by what I can only call 'a pitiful acceptance.' You haven't been worn down yet." The humanoid paused and turned toward the prisoners. "I know what you are and where you come from. Trust me when I say that turning you over to the F.P.U. will be better for everyone," he said.

"Now that you're here, you can't go back to that idle life—just waiting to die. Waiting for it all to be over. Yes—it will be more humane to turn you over to them. If you were to attempt elusion," he whispered thoughtfully, "the suffering would be greater than you could ever imagine."

With that Falin leapt up and clung to one of the thick cables, snorting briefly and then quickly vanishing into the gloom. The remaining hybrids surrounded them dutifully, stunners drawn. Orion groped for Chiu and Carla. He found them in a corner, silent, seemingly tranquil as the hybrids closed in.

Chapter 9

Having been the daughter of an F.P.U. dock loader (one of the lowest positions allotted citizens actually living at Headquarters), the fact that Sonja Lewin now held the distinguished rank of Chief Research Officer was nothing short of miraculous. At the age of twelve, she was the Head of Supplements' most trusted Twilight (a narcotic aptly named for its ability to keep the user in a perpetual state of hallucinatory transition) dealer. It had been easy to transfer and distribute in those days, as it was virtually indistinguishable from the plexifab that composed over ninety-eight percent of all vaccu-resistant materials.

Her closest childhood friend, Aurora, the only daughter of the billionaire that had first introduced plexifab to the Union. One night, she jokingly proposed to Aurora's father that he distribute the illegal substance by blending it with the resilient synthetic. He laughed loudly at the youngster's boldness.

But she had planted the proverbial seed. As reluctant as the tycoon had been to admit it, the suggestion was nothing short of genius.

The next morning he rooted through his list of contacts at the F.P.U. Twilight control unit. He reported that he had learned, in a desperate attempt by a terminated employee to salvage his position as Head of Manufacturing, of a dealer that had sold the translucent drug via sheets of plexifab. To further investigate, he deemed it crucial to interrogate a distributor that was being held in lock-up.

With all recording devices switched off, the entrepreneur guaranteed the inmate a full pardon if he could name the core supplier.

That's how it all began. Aurora's father acquired a large amount of Twi—its underground designation—and forged his empire. Billions of dollars snowballed into trillions, and Aurora's father managed—through a variety of unsavory dealings—to purchase the majority stock that comprised the Five Planet Union.

People came to crave the hallucinogen; by most accounts, even more-so than the long sought after habitable planet. The mobs clutched at the landing gear of overwhelmed distribution ships, snapping the drug up greedily like newborn chicks waiting for mangled bits of worm.

Once it penetrated their cerebrospinal fluid the work was done.

The pale mass retreated into its own "pseudo-Earth" and withered into skeletons that satisfied only their most basic needs.

Then Aurora's father—the richest man in the system and supreme crime lord—died while trying to seduce a prostitute aboard a mercenary ship. The sim-vids reported that he had been stabbed ten times by a malfunctioning Shultz. No more converters were programmed for defense after the incident.

Before his death, though, the man had provided Sonja with access to whatever she wanted at Headquarters. Many of her initial assignments were masked as internships, but when a position on the Official Union Directing Board opened, she expressed her desire to advance.

She was not refused.

This, of course, accounted for her present situation: lying prostrate and numb beneath the conference room viewing window. She didn't know why she had wanted this job in the first place. Likely it had much to do with occupying a position of power.

"But," she mused aloud between strained breaths, "Power over what? The tattered remains of a once thriving civilization?"

She didn't know.

Nevertheless, it was now her duty to inform the Union Board that Headquarters would have to be moved hundreds of millions of miles to the only place they'd have enough time to cobble together some harebrained escape plan.

Pluto.

Dr. Silvagno found himself stumbling toward the conference room. He discovered that the food scattered across the floor had been removed. There, below the seemingly opaque window, lay Sonja Lewin. It was then, amid a tranquility that seemed absurdly misplaced, that he was truly able to appreciate the woman's features for the first time.

Her was skin was fair; nothing about her was sickly or unnaturally taut. Her cheeks were flushed and pink; ripe.

"You realize we can't stay here," he said in his most authoritarian voice.

"That rift you've created will swallow this planet. And it will do it much faster than you think."

Deep Space Theory was a class that anyone wealthy enough to attend the F.P.U. Academy of Quantum Physics was required to take. He remembered many of the key topics well. Black holes occupied the first third of the semester, and he realized that this was actually only the fifth (or was it sixth?) time a person had actually witnessed the anomaly firsthand. To be more precise, it was only the fifth or sixth time someone had directly observed its *effects*.

"You need to issue a warning to the colonies," he said. "Any poor bastard who wanders into Neptune space, especially after a few more days, will be obliterated before they have any clue what's happened. It will only grow with a fuel source this steady."

"I know," Sonja said in an irritated tone. "Don't talk down to me. I attended the School too. Or don't you remember?"

Try as he might, the doctor found himself at a loss. They could only be two or three years apart in age, he guessed, but he had absolutely no recollection of her.

"We were in Deep Space Survival together," she continued hastily. "It was a small class that year."

Suddenly it dawned on him. Sonja—who was no longer the acne-covered swathe of hormones he now recalled in such great (albeit gruesome) detail—had blossomed into something almost completely unrecognizable.

"My God," he said under his breath. "It can't be..."

"It is," she said angrily. "It's good to see you too, Eugene."

Before he could respond Sonja was gone, stomping down the now empty hall, muttering inaudible complaints as she went.

He wasn't upset that he had caused her to leave. Eugene knew all too well the kind of person she was. "Besides," he whispered, "I'll be dead in less than twenty-four hours."

Pressure seized his chest. Gushkewau', for some unknown reason, had transformed into a python and tried to wrench the life out of him. Maybe it had been passing the very door in Eugene's mind as it swung open when he contemplated killing this "thing" that steadily consumed him. There was no way to be sure. For all of his agony, though, it seemed a glimmer of hope.

If it had read his thoughts, then it didn't like what it had seen. And so far Gushkewau' hadn't ever really been able to control him—to actually manipulate his physical actions long enough to make a difference.

Then a thought occurred to the scientist: why hadn't it left him and taken over Lewin? She could give it access to anything and everything it desired.

It had to know this.

Or, at the very least, why hadn't it spread itself into both him *and* her like it had the panicked fauna on 491? He didn't know, and this uncertainty bothered him.

His ribs constricted violently. The invisible vice wrung him mercilessly.

"I have to do it now," he breathed.

"Right now. Before it kills me."

*   *   *

Orion could barely see the rivulet of blood oozing from Chiu's nose. Just before they were bound and toted along the ceiling at a frightening pace, she had screamed.

He moved over to her, his wrists and ankles raw from the monofilament they bad been bound with.

"What happened?" he asked gingerly.

She unzipped and lifted the waist flap of her under-suit. He saw a bruise that looked like a peony on her side. Ori had barely made contact when Chiu began howling. It surprised Carla, who was in her own corner, trying feverishly to pry a ventilation grate out of the floor.

The researcher moved closer to the wound and saw that it wasn't a bite as was his first suspicion. It was a perfect circle—the center darker than the rest.

She had been injected.

His first thought was a tracking beacon. If the hybrids delivered her to the F.P.U. and provided her with the tools necessary to escape, she would be worth even more the second time she was apprehended and returned.

It was a sound theory, but something just didn't ring true.

"I think the hybrids injected you with something," he said plainly. "I don't know what."

Almost as soon as he had uttered the word, Orion knew. "Hybrids."

The mutation would likely begin in a matter of hours. No doubt the serum was already hard at work, extracting and replacing key sequences of DNA.

"They don't like to be called 'hybrids'," a voice croaked from a jagged hole high on the right wall.

"They prefer Homo Canidae. You know, like it's a real species,"

A prolonged silence stifled the small cell and was just as quickly crushed.

"ROVERS!" the man bellowed. "Yes—I call them Rovers." The voice drifted away from the hole. Notes of dry laughter swam in the must.

Orion darted to the location of the unseen informant. He unclasped a chair from the floor in the center of the room and stood, on his toes, peering through the crevice.

The cell of what he assumed to be a fellow captor was much darker. It was so dark, in fact, that impossible colors began to move like muted sunspots before him. He shut his eyes and massaged his forehead.

When his sight had adjusted, Ori saw a pair of luminescent eyes peering through the crack. They were very much like those of the Rovers. These eyes had a distinctly human quality, though, and they appeared at least partially amiable—not nearly as round and cold as the ones he had first glimpsed an hour earlier.

"Who are you?" Orion asked quietly.

The eyes, twinkling like a binary system, moved closer until they were just outside the fissure.

"The name's Orvice," he replied. "And who are *you*?"

"Orion Esocrat."

"Orion," the man repeated, "That's a nice name. I like it. I really do. Well, Orion Esocrat, I've been here for maybe two—two and a half months."

Orion already knew what he was going to say. Orvice was a drifter, like thousands of others, whose ship had been violently plucked out of intersystem space by the fabled mutant pirates. For some reason, Orion couldn't bear to hear the story. He just wanted facts.

"When did they give you the serum?"

Startled, Orvice moved away from the opening. "Yesterday," he finally said. "They kept me in here, in the dark for all that time, and then stuck me yesterday."

"Why did they wait so long?" Orion asked softly.

"I don't know. I guess because they wanted to get as much information from me as possible. They wanted to know who my friends are: *where* they come into port; *when* they come into port; *everything*."

The eyes turned away and were momentarily shielded by a bony hand.

"Now," he continued, "They've done this. They'll let me out of this cage soon enough, but I can't leave. I know that. Once it takes hold of you, that's it. You're not welcome anywhere else."

"There are probably a dozen more ships like this one," Orion thought. "Hell, maybe four dozen." And they need the monetary edge that can only come from dealing in illegally acquired scrap goods—metals, plexifab, philidium—the whole gamut. The Union was too self-absorbed to care about space monkeys and, really, why would they need to worry?

They wouldn't. If the F.P.U. perceived that the Rovers were a threat, they would, without question, be systematically sought out and destroyed. That, of course, would never happen, because the Rovers provided a necessary service that the Union didn't want anyone to know about. The interplanetary collective can't look weak in any way.

"Did you like it?" Orvice broke in. "It's a good joke, isn't it? Dogs, I've heard, used to be called 'Rover.' Not all of them, but most. That's what I've heard, anyway."

"Yeah," Ori murmured absently.

He looked down at Chiu and saw that she trembled.

In a moment of absolute quiet, he heard her teeth grinding. There were several poignant *cracks*. Carla had given up on the vent and sat eyeing her fellow prisoners.

Thinking back to his youth, a time temporarily spent stowed away in the bowels of a plush freighter where he encountered some of the most vivid characters ever to work the mines, he had come to a conclusion.

A little Twilight every now and then wasn't always a bad thing.

Chapter 10

Sonja Lewin was in a stupor when she dialed in the order to relocate Headquarters. She had barricaded herself in her condominium and removed a thin sheet of plexifab from underneath the deflated mattress in the guest bedroom. After igniting a single burner on her stove, she placed the transparent material in a pan and watched it bubble and warp.

Sonja was the only person allowed control of an open flame within the Headquarters complex. The oxygen level was high, and risk of burn out was a persistent threat. Only after allowing the maintenance Officials to install filters to balance the levels in her home was the ancient appliance installed.

When the substance had dissolved into an acrid puddle, she poured it through a funnel and into the empty capsules she'd prepared. Sonja then aligned them neatly on a shelf in her freezer. In three minutes they would be ready.

She slipped out of her undersuit and into a pair of "blue jeans" that she had obtained from a wealthy broker. The denim was thin and sloppily stitched together.

A "tee-shirt," which was entirely too big for her slender build, clung to her at the shoulders and swallowed her torso. It was gray, and, according to her sources, "moth-eaten," but she loved it, and didn't regret forking over five hundred thousand for it. Like the jeans, she deemed the garment irreplaceable.

It wasn't long before she had moved to the freezer and removed two of the capsules. She put one under her tongue and let the other slide effortlessly down her throat. The casing split open and the pill's contents coated her esophagus. She clutched a chair and felt the gravity shift; then there was the tingling, radiating first in her lungs, then, slowly, permeating the claw of her ribcage. The familiar numbness followed.

Her eyes fluttered, and she barely managed to punch in the access code for the intercom system.

"Ladies and gentleman," she said absently, "Secure your belongings. There's a problem. It's only minor, you see..." She giggled and cleared her throat. "But it's not all that safe for us to stay here. We're moving to Pluto."

She signed off and dialed the bridge of the West tower.

"It's time, Captain. Realign the engines. Let's get the hell out of here."

With a dull whine the com-link clicked off and she heard the robotic sound of gears churning. She dug into the wall padding of her apartment with her fingernails and braced for the initial thrust.

The compound rocked violently, and then there was a low moan. She ventured over to the extended window of her living room and watched Neptune transform into a distant electric marble.

Sonja collapsed against her oak armoire and, the pink rays now bathing her nightstand entered a Sun-soaked cantina. A fat man was serving cold beer in brown bottles. Beautiful women tossed bleached hair over their shoulders and smiled at the men sitting at the bar. Most were unable to smile back; they were preoccupied with swatting at the flies orbiting the remnants of half-eaten burgers.

The sound of the nearby Atlantic lulled her into a trance. Saltwater roared and foamed, the cool green of each wave tugging at her subconscious. She trotted carefully around an array of sandcastles that had been constructed by screaming adolescents. A crab, red, almost the color of rust, darted out of a small hole in the waning surf and scampered sideways across mulched shells. It was missing one of its legs.

Sonja studied the crustacean carefully—there was something sacred in its movement. Careful not to make direct contact with the black eyes, high on their stalks, she glanced, as nonchalantly as possible, as the thing was rolled over by the tide.

Along the beach was a row of crouched bungalows, each peering, like watchdogs, out across the ocean, deep into the rolling clouds where the horizon blurred into oblivion. Her jeans were warm, but not hot. The abundance of light fatigued her. She found a place in the sand that was cool. Music, drifting to her from the cantina, was overwhelmed by the offshore breeze.

Sonja then descended into a deep sleep.

Eugene hadn't packed anything. There was no need. He sealed the door to his room and made his way down the hall, weaving in and out of panicked residents desperate for answers. His body ached. Someone shouted from behind.

"Doctor! Please! You have to tell us. What's going on? What has happened?"

He didn't feel like a doctor. The title had lost almost all of its meaning for him. All of the knowledge he had acquired was now nothing more than freshly split firewood to be burned, ruthlessly devoured, for the beast inside. The thought sickened him.

"I don't know."

He hated lying. He had always wanted the truth, and despised actions that delivered anything else. Now, in his last moments of life, he was purposefully deceiving this terrified citizen whom he'd never met.

"Perhaps an Expansion," he said, his hands gesturing in wide arcs. There it was again: the lie. But it didn't matter. What *would* the truth do for these people? It would likely send them spiraling further into a state of uncontrollable panic, and nobody needed that. What he needed was to get to the nearest transport and to begin the launch procedure.

Approaching a less traveled side corridor, protected by its large OFFICIAL EMERGENCY ONLY placard that dangled overhead, he directed the stampeding residents down a different hall and swiped the access card he had fished from Ms. Lewin's unzipped back pocket during her immature exit of the viewing room. He saw the gray card protruding, begging to be plucked, and knew it would gain him access to whatever he wanted in Headquarters. She always had two cards on her at any one time. It was something he had noticed at the conference. She habitually thumbed it as she spoke, sliding it silently back and forth along the curved edge of the table, pretending to absorb his body language.

"It's something she has probably done all her life," he thought dully. Something to keep her face—*her mind*—occupied, so her expression wouldn't expose the lingering boredom.

Dr. Silvagno had noticed the second card jutting from her pocket at the same meeting. When she stood to leave, its thin coat of protective plexifab flashed in the overhead light.

In less than a minute, Eugene was onboard the transport. Clearly it was, as the sign had indicated, for "EMERGENCIES ONLY." There was barely room for him to stretch out his legs. An illuminated control panel surrounded him like a halo. Directly ahead was the thick viewing shield.

"Designed for atmosphere reentry," he mused. "Built to withstand heat."

"This thing must be a hundred years old," he whispered bleakly. The only atmospheres left for the vessel to penetrate belonged to planets (and some moons) that people no longer visited willingly.

The doctor located the ignition switch, and, closing his eyes, flipped it.

A shrill hum resonated from below.

There was an ominous clicking; circuits and processors sprang to life.

Thank God.

"System ready. State destination," the transport's nav-system said dryly.

"Neptune."

"Does not register. Please repeat destination."

Annoyed, he barked his response, this time more loudly: "NEP-TUNE!"

Belts automatically arced across his chest and lap, clamping him into place. The humming grew steadily louder, and, with an unexpectedly loud explosion, Eugene found himself plastered into the cushion.

Dr. Silvagno managed to turn just enough to see, out of the far corner of the shield, Headquarters rapidly diminishing behind him. Its wide rows of thrusters blazed, propelling it dutifully toward the edge of the solar system.

* * *

Orvice had been silent for a long time. Orion assumed he had finally fallen asleep, likely slumped in the uncomfortable chair that was, no doubt, also placed in the center of his cell. The women had kept to themselves, chatting softly for hours, Carla trying her best to mitigate her friend's growing terror. There had been no visible changes, but Chiu's breathing remained erratic and she clutched at her side reflexively.

Carla eventually made her away across the polished floor to where Orion sat, kneading his temples, lost in thought.

"So," she said in a low voice, trying to bring him, as tenderly as possible, out of the recesses of his mind. "What exactly did you learn about scuttlebugs?"

The question took him by surprise. What *had* he learned? He wasn't sure. Facts. Statistics.

Useless data.

"Well," he started, "For one thing, they're not actually 'bugs' as so many people have assumed. That is, they're not giant insects. They're mammals. You'd be surprised at how many people don't know that."

She nodded and smiled, genuinely intrigued.

"I mean, really we were there simply to observe and record. They instantaneously transport—er, teleport—themselves to different points in the ice very often."

"How often?" she asked.

"On average," he said, peering up at the drab tangle of cables overhead, "Once every four minutes. It's a defense mechanism."

"Defense from what?"

"Each other," he replied bluntly. "There are far more males than females. There's non-stop competition for control of the pride. The male that emits the brightest, most luminescent flash during teleportation seems to be the most respected. It's what we've labeled the 'shock and awe' tactic," he said. "You know, they 'wow' them with it. It scares off others—and there really is a correlation between the luminosity of the teleportation sequence and survival. Usually it's only twenty or thirty feet, but some have traveled miles. This only happens when they're spooked."

"How do you know which one is teleporting where?" she inquired. "I mean, don't they all look the same?"

"Well, not exactly," he said, "There are small differences. Follicle color. Heat signatures. Markings where the tusks exit the mandible..."

Orion could see she was getting bored. For some reason, it annoyed him.

"There are several that we fixed with tracking devices," he concluded curtly. "We mainly just watch them."

"Tracking devices? How?"

He tried to smile at Carla and casually folded his arms.

"Modified converters," he replied, "That are equipped with heat generators—very powerful heat generators—that bore down into the ice and attach the equipment."

She moved closer to him and leaned against the wall with the crevice.

"That's interesting," she finally said, "But is there really any validity to what the F.P.U. is trying to do? Can scuttlebug cells really teach them how to teleport objects and—of course— people?"

Ori sighed. His body and mind had reached the point of complete and utter exhaustion. He didn't feel like answering any more of her questions. He started to protest, as politely as possible, but he saw a look on her face... a look that made him regain his composure and try, with all of his strength, to be what he had heard legions of ancestors (recorded, of course, on archaic sim-vids) refer to as "a gentleman." He realized he had to be making his first forefathers, now dead for centuries, extremely proud.

"Yes, I think there is," he said in conclusion. "Scuttlebug cells aren't carbon based. They contain some sort of unidentified, electromagnetic cytoplasm that allows them to teleport. Actually, a few months ago, the Union released a statement which said that 'top physicists' at the school on Io had determined the scuttlebug cells, with the appropriate charge, could cause inanimate objects to undergo the teleportation process. The basic components of the cells, of course, had been reconfigured mechanically—in the form of the Borsen engine."

Even when he was on Pluto, the F.P.U. provided him with their press releases. Carla stared at him through the muted blue, her lips pursed.

"The others—the prisoners, I mean—were provided with the press releases. I wasn't, because of my, well... my, you know, heritage."

Orion understood, but was skeptical.

"But didn't anyone tell you about what they have been doing? About what's been going on?" He turned to Chiu, whose head bobbed as she drifted in and out of sleep.

"What about her? Your best friend, right?"

"We're really not that good of friends," she said dejectedly. "We're loyal to each other, because we have a common goal. But we're not friends." At this, she hung her head.

"The Officials informed the other prisoners, upon my arrival many, many years ago, that I wasn't supposed to be given any information about the developments in the system. They were... " she inexplicably trailed off.

"...Influential."

Carla began to shake, the cold of stillness and space seeping in.

"They didn't need much convincing, though. I mean, I am the reason for the destruction of Earth. Of *home*."

There was no denying it: Orion now felt deep-rooted pity for Carla Grayson.

"Grayson."

He repeated the surname in his mind, carefully and phonetically—"Gray-son"—separating the two words as though they were, by nature, wrapped in grim connotation.

"Hey," he said at last, "We really should get some sleep." She only nodded. The couple moved away from the wall and found a smooth spot on the floor. Removing his jacket, Ori spread it out, the sleeves forming a *Y*. Carla approached it drowsily and collapsed, both hands tucked neatly under her right cheek.

Then Orion slept. His last waking thoughts focused on Orvice. The researcher finally gave himself over to slumber entirely, allowing his speculation that the transformed humanoid in the next cell might also be asleep, hanging, upside down, from the gnarled fixtures overhead, to become an unavoidable reality.

Chapter 11

Sonja Lewin awoke to the sound of frantic knocking. She tried, with minimal success, to pull herself up and out of the stiff embrace of a faded armoire. Her neck was like iron, and she was unable to feel her legs.

The knocking grew louder.

The left leg of her jeans had torn during the fall she experienced when she began drifting out of consciousness. Sonja removed the garment with care and was soon standing in the undersuit so vital to maintaining warmth.

Lewin moved to the door and unlatched it.

A low-ranking official nodded and greeted her.

"Ma'am."

"What is it?"

"Pardon my intrusion, I know you like—"

Rolling her eyes, Sonja leaned against the aluminum threshold and stared at the man. He couldn't of have been older than twenty.

"Please. I've had a long day. Just get on with it."

"Right," he replied. "Dr. Silvagno has stolen a transport."

Sonja wasn't surprised. She caught herself smiling and sent the Official on his way.

Eugene had stolen a transport. So what?

She realized that his absence didn't bode well for the Union's media persona, but it didn't matter. He had made it back alive, and that was hope enough for everyone. Even if the Borsen project failed—which, she remembered sickly, it *had*—it was possible to make it to 491 by conventional methods. It would take a very long time, of course, but it could be done. That, at the very least, was something.

In Sonja's estimation, the F.P.U. wasn't a "bad" government. It had its fair share of corruption, but the government was still made up of people. "And," she mused, "People are basically good."

Every person that was still alive wanted one thing—to perpetuate the species. It was something inherent; the most basic of instincts. According to all of the models that had been published since the initial Expansion, the human race should've withered away long ago. The fact that they had adapted to life floating through a merciless void was, she realized, a testament to mankind's will to live.

Still, the government wasn't omniscient. It was merely a symbol: a manifestation of "leadership" and "guidance" among a tattered civilization.

In the most direct sense of the word, it wasn't "necessary." People, in all likelihood, could survive independently—especially since the majority that now lived existed only because their ancestors had possessed the wealth and self-preservation intuition to abandon Earth for deep system space before it was too late. Somehow, they had the resources to make it in a universe where all odds were against them.

The ones that congregated at the fringe saw it fit to create the Union. They postulated that it would help preserve the smallest shred of what they referred to as "humanity"—to demonstrate, if nothing else, that they were more than cockroaches scattering under the sudden appearance of a scorching kitchen light.

They wanted to feel like they were still in control.

But that was the point. They weren't in control; to consider that a possibility was naïve. A few bits of salvaged technology were the only things holding it all together.

And here was this pale descendant, halfway between two planets, inching pitifully toward the brink of the heliosphere.

The intercom above the sink flashed brightly. She moved to it wearily and saw that it was the Captain.

"Yes?" Sonja asked in a disconsolate tone.

"Ma'am," he responded, "I think it's important that we issue some sort of warning about entering Neptune space. Several of the other Board members agree. We don't want any unnecessary loss of life. It won't look good. Reports from ships trying to locate Headquarters—and not finding it— will spread rapidly..."

The Captain trailed off and static crackled momentarily.

"Anyway, I need your permission to send the transmission."

Sonja didn't know what to say. If the warning was sent, there would be questions. Lots of questions. She wasn't sure if she had the energy to conjure up a story about why they needed to leave Neptune; but, Lewin acknowledged, it would mean the end of the Union if she came out with the blunt truth.

She gave it a half-hearted test run:

"May I have your attention please? Yes: you. There's no one else, is there? The Borsen transporter has failed. Not only did it fail, but it failed miserably. And when I say 'miserably,' I mean that your cherished government has torn a hole in the space-time continuum and, according to the accepted theories of the past seven or eight hundred years, our solar system is now in its death throes."

The flair of static emanating from the white speaker reminded her that the Captain waited for a coherent response to his original question. She held the button and said grimly, "Send the warning."

"Yes ma'am. It will take several hours to reach most of the vessels that are equipped with our receivers, but I'm transmitting now."

It was done. Perhaps it was the large amount of Twilight she had just absorbed into the various segments of her brain stem, but she decided that people should know *something*. For years, she had protected the image of the F.P.U., but she knew this event couldn't be escaped. The entire Headquarters was relocated from the orbit it had maintained for decades. Things had irreparably changed.

"The questions," she mumbled. The fleet of wandering craft would immediately set course for the now absent capitol. She was certain the other Board members would have her do the explaining—she was, after all, the best with words. Her penchant for public speaking had played no small role in her ascent.

Sonja decided that she would tell them the truth, but gloss it—"doctor it up," so as to mask the horrifying truth of the disaster that it most certainly was.

"It was only an initial test," she contemplated reporting. "We have another transporter in the works. The best researchers on Io are hammering out the details as we speak." Confidence returned to her, and she brushed a strand of hair from her eyes. Then she remembered the news from the messenger.

Dr. Silvagno had stolen an escape pod. She mulled over this fact for several minutes. It didn't shock her, but the question remained: Why would Eugene do such a thing? He was the savior of the solar system. What would he gain? The more she sorted through the scenario, the less sense it made.

"He was always an oddball," she told the refrigerator. Eugene was the most enthusiastic scholar in regards to the radical notions of eleventh and twelfth dimensions. The memories of his incessant commentary on the subject bored her.

Maybe he was trying to reach "deity" status. Maybe he couldn't take his humanity with him into the interstellar reaches. Maybe he had to keep it where it belonged, with the bourgeois who, in all reality, never had a real chance of making it out anyway.

Sonja's thoughts turned to the Scuttlebug worshipers on Europa. "Maybe," she said glumly, "He's going to replace that giant worm."

Lewin told the kitchen computer to begin brewing a pot of coffee. She leaned against the counter and spoke loudly.

"Those damn researchers love that kind of stuff."

*   *   *

Eugene was cold. He had surfed the stars his whole life and still hadn't found a way to shake the feeling of bitter cold that insisted on encroaching *everything*. He was still hundreds of thousands of miles from Neptune when the booster powered down.

That's how the old transports worked. There was just enough propellant for the pod to achieve reasonable velocity, and that was it. It was a highly criticized idea by some of the early fuel conservation activists, but, Dr. Silvagno now realized, it was ingenious. Since there was no friction, once the pod achieved top speed there was no need to continue burning fuel. The sheer physics of traveling in a vacuum made it a no-brainer.

The doctor knew that he would soon have to contend with the transport's nav-system, which would try to adjust for the fact that the Headquarters was no longer where it should be. It would likely sound the alarm and fire all four thrusters at full power until the pod sat idle above the giant pulsing orb.

"Hopefully," Eugene said quietly, "The event horizon will have widened. It's probably just beginning to rip into the atmosphere. In a few more hours, it should be strong enough to pull me in from—"

The familiar tightening in Dr. Silvagno's chest caused him to cringe.

Then it left him. Eugene lifted his visor and took deep, halting breaths. Gushkewau', in its dark, gaseous form, emerged, filling the pod with its pallid vapor. Eugene gasped as the last remnants of the creature streamed from his body.

"Dr. Silvagno." It was the first time he heard its voice outside of his own mind. And, he realized, he didn't really *hear* it; more accurately, he felt it. The being spoke in baritone vibrations that shook the rusted control panel.

"Thank you for providing me with passage to the singularity. It would've taken me weeks without your assistance.

"Since we have reached our destination, I will now exit. I've never enjoyed viewing planets from behind mechanical confines," he said flatly. "My time with you has been more than educational, but, in case you were wondering..." he continued thoughtfully, "From what I've seen of other systems destroyed by their anchor stars, your species will probably be extinct within the next one-hundred forty years."

A low sound shook the doctor, and he was suddenly seized by fear. This Gushkewa' meant to leave the transport *now*. He could feel it, and the thing had stated as much.

The instrument panel once again rattled; slowly at first, and then with increasing intensity. Arcs of white electricity crested the nav-system's CPU to his right. "Thank God they stopped filling these things with pure oxygen," the doctor thought dumbly.

Shakily, Eugene lowered and sealed his visor.

The canopy of the transport blew open, and he was yanked out of the cockpit. Pieces of the small shuttle were sent spinning off in every direction, glittering like shards of stained glass in the neon hue of the bulbous Sun. His vaccusuit sensed his exposure and immediately began pumping air into his helmet. The emergency coils sprang into action, too, and the heat soothed him. It radiated from the area surrounding his sternum and the numbness soon disappeared.

Then there was only the sound of measured breaths and muffled calculations.

Dr. Silvagno located what was left of the escape pod as it, several seconds behind schedule, began flashing its yellow emergency lights. It was already a tumbling scrap heap; by the time he considered using his thruster pack to try and jettison toward it, he knew the distance was too great.

Eugene was about to die.

Without realizing it, he had entered Neptune's orbit. The doctor prayed he was in the vicinity of where Headquarters had been located. He knew the odds of such an occurrence were unfathomably low, be he prayed; the doctor squeezed his eyes shut and babbled steadily.

Then he blinked.

There were no ships in sight. Only the vague, infrequent glint of stars millions of light years away, made soft by the sea of infinite blue unfurling like a colossal sapphire below, gave him an abstract sense of comfort.

Adams was gone. In fact, there were no more rings at all. Dr. Silvagno looked on as a small spot in space siphoned a turqoise line of methane from Neptune's atmosphere.

So this was the fate of a planet that had existed for billions of years. It was being eaten by a science experiment gone awry.

To his astonishment, Eugene was then able to make out the form of Gushkewau' as it sailed toward the black hole, parts of its gaseous composition trailing like the nebulous leftovers of a recently deceased star.

He asked his vaccusuit how much oxygen remained.

"Seven minutes."

It was long enough to reminisce about Sonja Lewin and how the awkward face and arms she possessed during their college years had been majestically transformed by age.

Age! Of all things! "What a rarity," he thought absently. He knew Lewin's beauty was natural when he first saw her at the conference table. No plastic surgery, even performed for the most prominent of Board M.D.s, could be that convincing.

"Few people are ever that lucky," he said softly, his breath causing the visor to fog. "Very few."

"Five minutes of air remaining," his vaccusuit reported dully in a factual female voice. "Replacement pack needed immediately."

Dr. Silvagno prepared to unclamp his visor, and see, once and for all, if being exposed to the vacuum was what he imagined it would be.

An object, blinking vaguely in his peripheral, stopped him.

It was a ship. Not F.P.U., though. He wasn't surprised about that—he was an important symbol for their success, but not that important. They wouldn't risk following him back to this location.

The craft had strange markings along its hull—something like hieroglyphs. As it drew near, he was able to distinguish the characters. They were scribbled somewhat unevenly, as if they had been applied with the elegance and sophistication that only a four-year old can muster.

It was an ancient text.

The vessel's searchlights gleamed. Then, when the hatch opened and the hunched figures floated toward him toting restraints, he was afforded a clear view.

The text was written in what had come to be known as Babble.

It read, quite simply, "The Ark."

*   *   *

Chiu was conscious long before she felt the engines power down. Her eyes were sore, but, she suddenly realized, her vision was now greatly improved. Her pupils cut through the surrounding darkness involuntarily—she could see the tangled highway overhead with vibrant clarity. It was a series of metal pipes that had once been, she could tell from the worn paint, a frequently traveled route. As a matter of fact, there were two openings that had been welded shut where the wall joined the ceiling at both ends of the room.

Stretching, she tested her flexibility. Her side throbbed, but she felt much better—more alert; more attuned. Chiu squatted, preparing to pounce. The muscles along her calves and thighs rippled, causing her to grate her teeth and balance on the balls of her feet. Suddenly, as if she were spring-loaded, Chiu soared upward and found herself dangling from the artificial bramble.

She dug in with her feet and discovered that her toes were prehensile. She was frightened. Chiu shivered, clutching anxiously at the now sagging cables.

Below, she saw Orion stir and slowly shake himself out of sleep. He immediately noticed Chiu was gone.

"Chiu," he whispered worriedly, "Are you still in here?"

She watched him blindly feel out the boundaries of the room, helplessly checking every corner. Then, as quietly as she could, she called down to him.

"Orion."

Immediately Ori jerked his head toward the ceiling, trying his best to make sense of the darkness before him. Chiu watched his eyes, waiting for that moment of recognition where he would be able to grasp the fate of his fellow fugitive.

That moment finally came, and Orion seemed much calmer. He backed into a corner and called up to her.

"Does it hurt?"

Perhaps reflexively, Chiu's right hand felt for the wound at her side. It was sore, but not unbearably painful. She realized that a layer of fine hair now covered the wound. Cautiously, she brought her fingers to her forehead. She felt the slope, the prominent brow—it felt dense, impenetrable. Chiu decided she could shatter, with a strategically placed head-butt, a solid block of marble if so directed.

The knowledge that she would never again be a "human" caused her grip on the cables to loosen. Internally, whatever that meant, she knew she would remain Chiu—the rebellious prisoner/miner sentenced to forty years on Pluto, who spent hours daydreaming about the luxurious prisons of Earth and what they might have been like.

Long ago she had obtained a sim-vid from an inmate named Sheldon Braddock. It was a display, and brief tutorial, about a historic landmark known as Alcatraz; "The Rock," as it was referred to in the pixelated holographic documentary. There was a segment that showed the cells themselves: simple, concrete cubes with doors that slid on hinges. "Primitive," she remembered noting, "but effective."

"Not as effective as the void," she concluded bleakly, hanging some fifteen feet overhead.

"What?" Orion asked, puzzled, rubbing his eyes and trying to identify her figure in the emptiness.

Her mind raced and she felt dizzy. Obviously, her anatomy hadn't completely adjusted to the changes so violently grafted to her DNA. The serum had worked well, but she doubted that it was finished. If that were true, the rest of the experience would be something she wouldn't have to adapt to: the constant motion, swinging from cables and pipes, constantly fighting to keep vertigo at bay.

"Listen," Ori said as quietly as he could, trying not to wake Carla.

"There has to be a reverse-serum; an antidote. It can be fixed. We just need to get out of here. Since you're up there, you can tell," he continued, "If the path you're on ever had an entrance in or out of here. It'll probably be welded shut."

Orion was always thinking, and Chiu admired that about him. He was absolutely right. There was, at one time, an entrance and an exit into the cell, but, she concluded, it didn't matter.

There was no antidote.

Just as her legs inherently knew the correct amount of tension to apply to her calves to overcome the one hundred-eighty inches that separated her from the ceiling, she knew an "antidote" didn't exist. It was inborn. Instinct.

Below, Orion paced impatiently, and Carla began to stir.

"You have to check," he said edgily. "Is there a way out of here?"

Chiu became annoyed. The feeling that Ori would now take advantage of her deformity to escape this place, and leave her and her newly adopted race to rot, gnawed at her gut. Anger boiled over, and she snarled rabidly.

Ori stopped pacing.

Chiu's eyes shone brightly for an instant. She knew Orion saw them.

She wouldn't acknowledge it initially, but there was a seed of bitter disdain concerning this particular researcher; it had been planted deep in her psyche, since the moment they first met, and had now, seemingly out of nowhere, unfolded into a black-petal rose of full-blown hatred. The way Carla looked at him—Carla, who had always been so dependent on Chiu's intuitiveness and inexorable yearning to leave Pluto—had found a new hero.

It was something that Chiu had suspected was true the first time she saw her companion smile at him on the Union ship as they departed Europa. Now her best friend, who had feigned remorse at the sight of her hideous transformation as she lay, convulsing on an alien floor, had abandoned her.

Her eyes disappeared. Ori crouched on the floor, his arms tense, ready for impact.

Chiu moved swiftly across the cables, plowing the rusty embankment that used to be an entrance to the cell with all of the force her forehead could muster.

It was a sickening sound. Carla was fully awake now, sliding slowly over toward Orion, trying to make sense of the chaos taking place overhead. With each thud, Chiu moaned loudly, and outside the room the Rovers approached, their brutish language eventually drowning out the rhythmic banging. Without warning, the ancient alloy lost its hold on the wall and separated. Green light filtered in through the cleft, and Ori was able to see Chiu's silhouette. She hung, like a weary bat, staring down at them.

Then she was gone. Orion helped Carla get to her feet, and they took a moment to stretch and exhale. He didn't realize how long he had been holding his breath.

The barking sounds of Rovers faded, as, Orion presumed, they chased Chiu down the hall she had breached. Carla began to cry softly.

Ori didn't say anything. He tried to hug her, but it was no use. She dabbed at her face weakly.

"Everything all right, neighbor?"

Orvice waited at his crevice. "It sounded like they started construction on a new wing of the ship," he said jokingly.

Orion peered through the crack and saw Orvice's eyes staring back jovially.

"Well, I'll be," he said. "It looks like you've had someone bust out, eh?"

Looking over his shoulder, Orion realized the hybrid could see the gaping hole at the junction of wall and ceiling. The light, though minimal, poured through and was exaggerated by the intense black. Now that he had a clear look at it, the cell wasn't as bad as Ori had originally thought.

It was plain. That's all. There wasn't anything to become comfortable on, which, he postulated, was the whole point. And, even more importantly, there wasn't anything to use as a weapon. Still, even though he doubted it would do much good as a tool of blunt force, there was the solitary chair. Orion was able to see now that it had been fastened with metal braces—corroded ones—just as weak as the patchwork sheet Chiu had recently decimated.

"Hopefully very weak," he mumbled. Chiu, he had gathered from observing the other Rovers, sported a solid inch-to-two-inch plate of bone designed to withstand a significant impact. This, he postulated, is what she had used to remove the jagged piece of metal.

Ori wasn't as well-endowed.

He had skinny arms, a back arched with the beginnings of scoliosis, a weeping companion, and an unstable Rover laughing hysterically in the other room.

Orion cleared his mind and decided he had better find a way to make use of the chair.

And he realized he had better find it fast.

Chapter 12

She neatly arranged five sheets of Twilight and slid them into her orange backpack. Sonja hadn't embarked on a binge of this magnitude for at least five years.

Even though her cognitive abilities had returned to normal, the substance still had its effects—and, after considering the rash, decidedly selfish actions of Dr. Silvagno, she decided it was her duty to intercept him. This, she rationalized, would be the only way she could redeem herself in the eyes of the Board.

Not that it really mattered. If she told them she wanted to gouge ten additional black holes in the space-time proximity of their diseased star in an effort to put it out of its misery— permanently snuff it out, because its relentless red made her, for lack of a better word, claustrophobic—they would protest, but, in the end, like everything else she demanded, her will would be done.

Groggily, she moved once again to the intercom mounted in her kitchen and flipped the switch for the bridge.

"I'm going out for a while. Don't wait up for me." Sonja laughed stupidly.

"Ma'am?" the Captain asked. "You're going out?"

"Yes," she replied tersely. "Eugene—Dr. Silvagno—has stolen a transport. That's F.P.U. property. I'm going to get it back."

"Ms. Lewin," the Captain responded, "I have several Officials en route to overtake the doctor. You don't have to—"

"Nonsense," she broke in, "I outrank you, don't I? I can handle this. Let them take a break. They do that kind of thing all the time. Parading across the outer system, policing what's left of humanity as if their lives depend on it."

Before the Captain could reply, she terminated the link. At the door of her apartment, she considered making the journey in the dilapidated jeans crumpled atop her wicker hamper (yet another of her unparalleled luxuries).

She climbed into her personal transport, which had remained docked at the rear entrance of her flat for the past two years without any use. Still, the mechanics had routinely flushed the fluids and updated the necessary components. Any time she wanted to go somewhere, a more secure ship, its hull dotted with turrets and the latest in plexifab plating, was sent to accommodate her.

Now, sinking into the crisp leather of the pilot's chair, Sonja realized she couldn't remember how to operate the damn thing. She glowered at the instruction panel that had been constructed for her, molded from pure silver and mounted alongside the newly installed nav-system, and struggled to execute the start-up procedure.

Clumsily, Lewin managed to free the rigid sphere from the underbelly of Headquarters. She unzipped her pack and ignited the mini-oven she had had retrofitted one year earlier.

The space station had almost completely vanished when she realized she had forgotten the all-important frying pan. In an unbridled state of panic, she searched the storage compartments for something—a pot, a plate, the underside of a well-polished cranium—*anything* she could use to melt the mind-freeing narcotic she so eagerly longed to consume. Then it hit her: the plaque.

Sonja ripped and pulled, greedily and with what little strength she had, at the gleaming set of instructions that explained how to operate her hydrogen-fueled series YU850 transport. The silver plate finally sprang loose with a piercing squeal.

Her eyes were like yolks in the dull yellow light.

She placed the plate on the burner. The raised lettering caused the iridescent substance to hiss as it curled around commas and semicolons. When it was finally ready for collection, Sonja noticed that it had begun to solidify around one sentence in particular:

"FOR TROUBLESHOOTING, SEE ABOVE."

*   *   *

Face to face with Rovers, Eugene found that he was at a loss for etiquette. They crowded around him, bobbing like buoys, grunting and scratching as he removed his helmet.

The fact that he wasn't dead surprised the doctor; even more surprising was the realization that he was glad he had survived.

On top of that, Gushkewau' had left him. His darkest hour had miraculously transformed into his most joyous.

Eugene was *free*. He thought about many things without fear of consequence.

His earliest memory of Rovers, a species that only the elite and the most unfortunate ever encountered, was in his elective at the University on Io—"Anatomy of the Enemy." They had been labeled "the enemy" because, quite simply, it was widely accepted that they couldn't be trusted. They were, in the most rudimentary sense, humans. Rovers contended with the same emotions, the same thoughts, the same desires; physically, though, they were extraordinarily different.

Really, they were superior to humans in many ways.

But, in the end, the consensus was that they were animals—wild, unpredictable.

Eugene now remembered Sonja more clearly. She was the one who had made the first incision across the abdominal cavity of the gaunt Rover corpse that lay beneath the sterile bank of lights in the lab. The woman had been in two classes with him—he was surprised he hadn't remembered it sooner, though it was possible that could memories were a side effect of occupation by such an otherworldly enemy.

The scalpel, polished and flawless, right down to the hair-width blade that sparkled in the overhead lamp, had made him finally take notice of the equally straight red hair that lined her shoulders.

He needed a worthwhile distraction.

Despite the contortions of her acne-riddled face, she had the most beautiful hair he had ever seen. It was fierce and poignant—he remembered the professor of that particular class, Dr. Vosco, referring to her as "quirky little Miss Ireland."

At first, he didn't get it. Dr. Vosco later explained that, in the old world, people from Ireland typically donned red locks (that, in many instances, bordered on orange). The gene for red hair was all but extinct, making Sonja that much more exotic.

Why Dr. Vosco referred to her as "quirky" was something that required no explanation. Sonja took pleasure (some labeled it pride, but those who watched her work knew better) in slicing open the once-living Rovers in her anatomy class. As she worked, her tongue—bright and pink against the tiles—stuck to her upper lip with unwavering tension.

And she smiled.

That's what Eugene remembered about her more than anything. When she made the first incision, two rows of perfect ivories were revealed. The carcass, having thawed for three days before being presented to the students for examination, produced an acrid odor in the otherwise spotless environment.

At first there was only a trickle. A few beads of crimson emerged from the ruler straight line and congealed like glue. When the retractors were utilized, it became—only momentarily—a gory mist. The first time Dr. Silvagno (then the wide-eyed, eager student referred to by his pals as "Gene") was sprayed with the blood, he covered his mouth and scrambled out of the lab. The taste of bile rose in his throat and he hurled half-digested supplements into a narrow trash bin near the elevator. Several students, on their way to other classes, exited the elevator shakily, regarding him with raised brows and curled nostrils.

Nothing like this ever happened with Sonja Lewin, though. She was a rock. She sliced and diced with the best of them, anxious to wrap her slender, freckled fingers around the innards of whatever exotic being the University could produce. Eugene tasted that burning hydrochloric compound rising in his esophagus again when

Sonja ripped the spleen from the mangled Rover. It slipped out of her hand and landed—*splat*—very harshly, like a dead fish, against the slick floor.

It wasn't so much the sight of it all that got to Eugene. Here, having just returned from the vomit-filled trashcan, the sound of a Rover's spleen flatly streaking the white tiles caused him to run out green and whimpering once again.

Soon Dr. Silvagno had regained his composure. He limped into the lab one last time, many of his classmates snickering like tweens.

Gene approached Sonja, careful to avert his eyes from the mutilated display.

"You see," she said to him in a trance, her hands moving swiftly, "Everything seems much more compact. Notice the way the liver, the gallbladder, the colon— they're all crammed into a ball," she said dryly, "It's almost like one big super- organ."

Eugene didn't look. He only feigned interest and stared past Sonja.

At the end of the day, he didn't think he could look her in the face. This girl, barely a woman, had plucked the guts, without hesitation, out of a Rover and seemed whole-heartedly undisturbed by all that she'd witnessed.

Though she was undeniably studious, it was *fun* to her. The smile, more adult than anything else on her post-adolescent face, was frightening.

He wanted to smile back, but couldn't.

Eugene wouldn't have admitted it then, but he was, in an almost intangible way, genuinely scared of her.

Once the Rovers had lifted him to his feet, Dr. Silvagno nodded to each of them in turn, acerbically thanking them for saving his life. One, which appeared older than the rest due to the flecks of gray covering his snout, shouldered through the crowd.

"I'm Fralin," he muttered. "And you are correct to be grateful."

Eugene stared at him blindly, unable to respond. Growls rolled through the welcome party.

"I didn't mean any disrespect," he finally said. "I just—"

"You *did* mean disrespect," Fralin interrupted. "You people from the F.P.U. You're all alike."

Eugene wasn't sure if he should answer or simply keep his mouth shut. He opted for the latter.

The Rovers moved in on him quickly and bound his arms. They walked him, with their apelike gait, down the cramped hall that bled into darkness.

"The smell..." he thought. "It's unbearable."

The doctor remembered the stench of the dead Rover being worse, though, and was momentarily glad there weren't slain hybrids lining the walls.

Or were there? He couldn't tell.

It was as if night had fallen.

It was as if he had suddenly been returned to 491.

Chapter 13

Twilight did its job well. Less than a minute after pouring the fluid—this time without the protective sheathe of a capsule—down her gullet, Sonja was beamed into infinity. Her neurons, firing erratically and grossly misinterpreting all sensory data, told her she was outside of her transport. She was strolling, recklessly and carefree, among the distorted binary star systems of the Sombrero galaxy, casually pausing in front of the now miniaturized globes of light to give them squarely planted kicks; to send them puttering off into the ever after.

Her mind raced. The celestial breeze—an absurdity, Sonja acknowledged as cerebrally as possible—carried her to the fourth annual Neptunian light festival.

Perfectly sculpted holograms that the Clonpulls had retrieved from newly-discovered planets dotted the air above the gasping audience. The ceiling, with its ornate depictions of Greek Gods reigning unchallenged over the five planets, provided a Sistine-esque backdrop. Zeus, his beard flowing and full, twirled Jupiter on one index finger. The deity looked like a Globetrotter, one of those legendary twentieth century athletes who could manipulate a "basketball" any way they saw fit.

It was an honor to even enter the Five Planet Union's Chandler Hall of Photon Entertainment. "Photon," she mused, "is a misleading word. It was too rigid. Too academic."

The entertainment itself was nothing more than the product of manipulated prism technology, it was true, but the images themselves were anything but simple rays.

They were real.

Her father, Walter Lewin, had his hair combed back neatly. It was also red. He smiled at her, his tuxedo worn and frayed. It had to be over sixteen years old. The muscles at his jaw tensed; it was a sign that he was overcome with joy. This was, after all, a luxury they hadn't often experienced. Since her mother had no real technological skills, or any ability that she could pass off as "necessary," she was required to stay at home. Women who had given birth at least once and remained in good health were to live untouched. The idea was that if a woman had already produced one child, the odds for another were good. Fertile women, Sonja remembered, were increasingly hard to come by.

Shiloh Onyx, her father's employer, emerged from the crowd with one hand extended. Walt and Shiloh greeted one another heartily, laughing and carrying on about an incident that had happened the day before.

"Sonja," Shiloh said coyly, "It's good to see you. The last time I saw you, you were *this big*." He held his right hand flat and horizontal, just above her collar. Sonja manufactured a polite smile. Overhead, the flickering beams continued to produce detailed holograms of canyons and rivers, rising and falling amid "oceans of peroxide," as the noble-voiced narrator phrased it.

Inexplicably, Mr. Onyx dropped his champagne glass onto the unforgiving floor at their feet and it shattered. Shards were flung in every direction, and the bubbling alcohol pooled in a dip. The honeyed liquid quivered amid the bass pumping from the walls.

Without hesitation Walter dropped to his knees and gathered the jagged pieces of glass in a purple handkerchief that had been tucked in his breast pocket. The clattering androids came to his aid, cheerily requesting that Mr. Lewin remain standing so that he could enjoy what was left of the show.

Sonja knew why he wouldn't get up. It was his inherent servitude—his desire to help others. He actually *enjoyed* being at the bottom of the food chain.

It made her furious. Sonja's mother encouraged him to let the waiters, now rocking idly at his side while he mopped up the champagne, carry out their directive. This was *his* night. Mr. Onyx had invited Lewin to the party as a Guest of Honor because of his "unmitigated devotion to the Union."

Walter refused. His hair, now disheveled, hung in greased clumps before his eyes, partially obscuring his vision. He brushed it aside angrily.

Sonja knew he didn't like this about himself—his inability to let others do the "lowly" things. But the man couldn't help it. It was a reflex.

An especially large shard of the broken goblet caught Sonja's eye.

She approached it cautiously. The jagged fragment had its own source of illumination. It seemed to throb.

The theatrics of the light show were soon an afterthought. All eyes were trained on the illuminated remnant she now held in a Statue of Liberty pose.

Then she saw that it was a star. No, not a star; a planet. It was a blue planet.

Neptune. Sonja was jolted back to her senses by the flat nav-system voice of her transport's computer.

"Proximity alert," it stated. "A sizable object is within impact distance of the hull."

She strained, her eyes still dilated under the weighty influence of Twilight.

"Firing reverse thrusters."

The shipped seemed to momentarily buckle, protesting with inanimate groans, but the planet still grew larger. She soon recognized the thin trail of debris that whirlpooled outside the thick plexifab.

Sweat appeared on Sonja's forehead in the weak light. Her hands shook. She felt the cold, nervous anticipation of someone who was about to experience something awful—something genuinely terrible.

And she knew there was nothing that could be done to stop it.

*   *   *

Orion had scrambled down from the newly-fashioned hole at the ceiling just as he heard the cell door unlock.

Carla sat silently, her knees pulled up to her chin. The door burst open and two Rovers hobbled in, their breathing gruff and labored.

Between them was a hunched figure—a human. That was clear immediately. His posture (the silhouette of his posture, anyway) was strikingly bipedal.

The Rovers dropped the man abruptly. With a shuttering clank, the door had been bolted and they found themselves alone with the stranger.

Rovers spoke, in throaty whispers, just outside the place where Chiu had smashed her way to what could only be a temporary freedom.

"I'm Eugene," the stranger said quietly. "Eugene Silvagno."

He sat not far from Carla, one fist propped underneath his chin.

"Orion Esocrat," Ori replied in an equally reserved tone. "And this is Carla Grayson."

Orion didn't see the point in concealing her identity. They were prisoners—there was no telling what the F.P.U. would do to them when they were returned to the complex. So, Ori decided, it would be best to have an ally if any escape attempt were to be made.

The thought caused him to chuckle.

"What's funny?" Eugene asked in an aggravated tone.

"Nothing. Well, I was just thinking about breaking out of here when, you know," he lowered his voice, "The right opportunity presents itself. It's ridiculous, I know. Only…"

He paused, surveying the room. "Only I can't go down like this. You know? Not like this. I haven't even done anything wrong. Well, that's not entirely true…"

Orion stopped speaking. He drew in a deep breath, and tried to locate Eugene's eyes. For some reason, he felt an urgent need to try and clearly discern the man's features.

"Sorry. I was rambling. I'm a researcher from Europa. A Scuttlebug colonist."

Eugene smiled, the feeble light momentarily reflecting off of his unbelievably white teeth.

"I'm a doctor. Not an M.D. A PhD. But that's beside the point. I came out here to kill something."

Orion grew cautious, his glare darting convulsively between Dr. Silvagno and Carla.

"Don't worry," the doctor said, sensing the tension. "I wasn't contracted by the Union. I'm no bounty hunter. Like I said, I'm a doctor. I was the one chosen to go to 491."

At this Carla drew her face and stared at the newcomer as if he had said he were Jesus Christ.

Ori laughed, though he tried to restrain it. His body loosened, and he stretched out on the floor.

"Really," he replied sarcastically. "Tell me, how's all that going?"

"Not well," Eugene said gravely. "This entire ship, along with the Rovers, you, me and Satan over there," he said, motioning to Carla, "are about to be compressed into an infinitely dense ball of matter and radiation."

With a sigh, Orion propped himself up.

"What the hell does that mean?" he asked, irritable, exhausted, only wanting to find a comfortable position for his aching hip.

"Look," Eugene continued, "I really did reach the planet. Don't think about what the F.P.U. has told you—block all of that out. I went there, to 491, and brought back a... *being*. Something organic, but, paradoxically, inorganic. It was living, you see, but not like us. It was—*is*—like an all-consuming fog. A black fog. That eats everything it sees. And the worst part is it knows more about us than we do... it knows more about *everything*."

Carla's posture stiffened, she tried to locate Ori's hand—something concrete to grasp.

Orion scratched his scalp with chewed nails. He examined, as best he could, Dr. Silvagno—this stranger. This man who claimed to be the savior of the solar system, the one the Union broadcasts proclaimed the hero of the millennium.

Eugene wasn't lying. Orion knew it from the tautness of his voice; the way the stranger's mouth remained fixed, narrow; resolute about preaching the truth. The doctor might have been insane, but at least he believed he was being honest.

Ori humored him as best he could.

"So this 'being,' whatever it is, isn't dead. Where is it then?"

Orion framed his next question as sarcastically as possible.

"Is it here *now*?"

"No," Dr. Silvagno said, audibly relieved, "No. But it was *here*," the doctor said, tapping on his chest.

Eugene flexed his fingers, one arm outstretched before him, the black, virtually invisible palm almost touching Orion's face.

"It was *here* for a long time."

Rovers grunted, their animal growls penetrating the cell. Sparks rained down, and momentarily the cell was actually *too* luminescent. Before they could register a protest, the hole was patched. The darkness, once again, was absolute.

For a long time they sat in silence.

"What happened with the Borsen engine?" Ori nosed the question in as casually as he could.

"It malfunctioned," Dr. Silvagno said grimly.

"Malfunctioned?"

"Yes," he started again. "We're almost in it now, I'm sure."

"*In it*? What are you talking about?"

"It—"

He didn't finish. The ship shook, quietly at first. The reverse thrusters ignited and there was scrambling. Then, without warning, the craft jerked violently to port side.

Carla began panting, her wet, slick fingers pulling at Orion's undersuit.

There was a pressure; a stretching; a painful tenderizing and an overabundance of pure, white light. In horror, Ori watched the aluminum walls wither as if they were kindling. Silence pervaded everything, and his cellmates became waxen statues. The scene became an eternal Polaroid before they too were reduced to a series of quarks connected only by a previously undetected nineteenth dimension.

Then, as perception became a thing of the past, emptiness was the only reality.

PART TWO

Chapter 14

Orion's grandfather was overly nostalgic. The old man would coerce the pudgy eleven year-old, with promises of gumdrops and gummy bears (both genuine delicacies), into listening to him reminisce about the only "real" place in the solar system.

But that's how it was with Earth. Elderly people talked about it as if they had been there only two days ago. It was a place that contained something that almost everyone of Orion's generation was without; that most precious of commodities— identity.

"All this relocation," his grandfather said, "It's absurd. We should've gone down with the ship."

"Bullshit!" Orion heard him scream once. The word was etched into his brain. Ori's grandfather had never used an explicative in his presence, but, this one time, when he was particularly enraged about the displacement of humanity, he proclaimed it without reservation.

"Bullshit!" he said again, peering down at the boy's upturned nose.

"But it seems like I'm the only one who thinks so." The hunched figure turned feebly away from his grandson.

"We can't go on like this, Orion." He wandered over to his Tupperware box of sim-vids and selected one that was labeled "Documentary: EMPEROR PENGUINS."

The hologram was broken by deteriorated data, and the creatures inexplicably moved from one side of the diorama to the other when bits of dust obscured the reader.

Orion's grandfather plopped down in his green chair and sprinkled a handful of gumdrops into the boy's outstretched palms. The old man's lips twitched beneath a push broom mustache.

Ori sucked on the candy. He watched the snowdrifts rise, get blown away by sweeping arctic gusts, and subsequently coagulate into powdered mounds. The penguins hobbled about like lemmings, trying desperately to keep their delicate yellow eggs from making contact with the bleached surface. Orion sat transfixed as one of the eggs rolled, in an incredibly awkward fashion, from its mother's foot-cradle.

The thing split gruesomely on the ice.

Orion began crying. The pink gumdrop in his mouth tumbled, like the destroyed egg, onto the concrete floor of his grandfather's Neptune flat and stuck there noiselessly.

The old man grumbled something inaudible and quickly returned with a rag so he could pluck the saliva-coated chunk of sugar off of his otherwise spotless floor.

Ori's vision blurred and he strained to see the birds, huddled in groups in an effort to survive the elements, always—even then, on a living planet with an amiable atmosphere—so unforgiving.

"Forget it," his grandfather finally said, straining to rise to his feet. "It's not for a new generation. Nobody cares about Earth. Nobody cares about the old ways."

*   *   *

Eugene vomited loudly into the drain at the center of the cell. The sour stench spread across the room faster than any of them had anticipated. Carla tried to remain silent, pinching her nose and breathing heavily through her mouth.

The whole thing was surreal. For a split second Orion saw his cellmates vividly, their every feature outlined in a lustrous concentration of electric light. It was brighter than anything he had ever experienced (that included his venture to the core of the solar system, his assignment to collect solar particles that were violently launched from the churning core of the crimson star).

He remembered watching Carla's eyes, dark, gaunt and yellow, almost as if they were stricken with jaundice, dissipate into billions of pixels that funneled into the unmolested luminosity.

Then this.

Nausea. Quivering. Overwhelming uncertainty.

After several minutes they were all feeling a little better. Orion had regained his sensibilities, his stiff heels scraping against the metal floor as the blood channeled a sense of temporal awareness to his brain.

"What the hell just happened?" the researcher asked hoarsely.

"We should be dead," Dr. Silvagno responded.

Carla broke in. "But we're not."

"So I noticed," he said matter-of-factly. The three of them sat in silence for several minutes. Rovers vaulted by outside the cell with loud, snarling leaps, their movements not as fluid as they had been only minutes before. They too, it seemed, had been caught off guard by... what?

"What did you mean 'We should be dead'?" Carla finally inquired in a stubborn tone. Her voice shook with impatience.

"They tested the Borsen engine for the first time about twelve hours ago." Eugene answered.

"And?"

"And it worked—though not like they anticipated."

She slapped the cold floor and wrung her hands.

Eugene continued as best he could.

"When they triggered the engine, it caved in on itself. Or at least I think it did. This is only speculation, mind you, but it's pretty educated speculation." He laughed apprehensively and went on to explain the results of the test—how the entire F.P.U. Board had been on hand for, well, nothing short of a colossal failure. He tried, with gentle adjectives and an excess of verbal padding, to soften the blow.

The ship had created a black hole. It was eating the solar system.

"And the Neptune complex," he added dryly, "Is headed to the outer edge of the system. They say to Pluto, but it will likely go farther."

Dr. Silvagno was quiet for a moment.

"They're going to eventually send a broadcast announcing their position," he concluded, "They'll want to draw in every transport, vagabond vessel, freighter— anything they can to siphon extra fuel. I imagine they'll collect it all for one last spectacular burn." He paused, listening intently. Eugene wanted them to ask him what he meant. He liked feeling important. It was something that had been viciously torn from him upon his exit of that very uninformative Board meeting on his first day back.

"To 491," he said in a deep voice. "They haven't told me this, but I think they're making a run for it. There aren't enough provisions for the rest of us to make it. It's only the elite..."

The doctor seemed on the verge of a history lesson, so Ori broke in.

"If the engine created a black hole, then why aren't we dead? I mean, we were within several hundred thousand kilometers of the Neptunian atmosphere when we picked you up, right?"

Carla peered in his direction, puzzled, trying to understand how he could've possibly known their location.

"Rovers," he said bluntly, "I heard them barking to one another before the hole was patched."

"I don't know," Eugene answered. "It doesn't make any sense."

"We couldn't have— "

"No," the doctor interrupted, reading his suggestion. "That's impossible."

Carla breathed softly, her hand clutching Orion's forearm. Soon, his nausea had left completely. All he could think about was this touch; this *human* touch. It was something he had experienced, only briefly, one other time in his life. When he wasn't thinking about Earth or the prospect of settling on QR-491, he thought about that one fleeting moment that had been tattooed on his brain decades ago.

Before he was shipped to Pluto, Ori met a woman named Mayulli Corum. He was swaying gently, nodding off in the cradle of a torn hammock he had purchased from a toothless vendor in the Complex. Others sat near him, playing cards, joking with each other coarsely. One word—an antiquated word—clung to his ear and caused him to open his eyes.

"Bitch!" one of the boys said after angrily Frisbee-ing a platter of supplements across the room.

"We ordered the chicken—remember, c-h-i-c-k-e-n," he insisted mockingly. The others laughed, their heads rocking back and swallowing generous gulps of air.

The boy who had caused the hard little pills to scatter and settle in numerous crannies in the recreation tank they occupied was not physically impressive. He had scrawny arms that hung awkwardly from a coat hanger clavicle. He was a disproportionate boy with a spongy build.

He was weak.

Orion had never been in a fight, but he was sure he could easily dismantle the wiry crane operator.

It wasn't so much the word—"Bitch!"—that had enraged him. It was the crane operator's malicious intent; his direction of it, fired with sweltering malevolence at what Orion knew was the most beautiful woman he had ever seen.

Mayulli bent over, humbly collecting the supplements, returning them to their designated slots in the plastic tray. He had seen her before, and had asked his best friend (and bunkmate), Rama, whether or not she was married. It was a ridiculous question. Hardly anyone married, but it was a practice that some clung to in an effort to preserve at least some remnant of the former traditions.

"No, Orion," Rama said plainly. "I don't really know much about her, though. She works in the cafeteria. You know, filling the supplements. She was lucky to get assigned here."

No joke, Ori remembered thinking. This was paradise compared to the asteroid harvest. In those days, saying that Pluto was the manifestation of hell was laughable—to get stuck on an asteroid, destroying your body for the sake of a government-designated pseudo-mineral, was akin to suicide. With rapidly spinning rocks, the gravity is nominal. Like horses, the workers were forced to wear blinders. These helped shield the constantly spinning stars from their field of vision. Without this, the vertigo would have been all-consuming.

Orion remembered a statistic he read once: 78% of the workers assigned to asteroid duty were usually flung off, like slippery cowboys on the backs of livid steer, into the gaping black.

But these thoughts about being decimated by a bucking piece of space rock were temporary. Mayulli was forever.

Ori turned the hammock on its side and he spilled out like the yolk of a freshly cracked egg. His sleep was shaken off by the sobering rage that coursed through him, fueled by what he perceived to be the most egregious, most ancient and certainly most cardinal insult of insults—the verbal slurring of the woman he loved. Orion planted his feet and tightened his fists.

The crane operator saw it coming. He flipped the table and absorbed the attack. Orion sank to the floor, the stringy arms of his opponent wrapped tightly around him. They rolled, clumsily, only for a moment, before Ori found himself with his back against the cold tile underneath.

Then came the stinging blows, one after the other, pummeling the mound of fat that clung to his left cheek. It was rosy by nature, but soon it was a dark red, split and dribbling steady red tributaries. They thickened with each punch. Orion lay there, helpless, watching through swollen eyelids as Mayulli raised a hand to her thin, brown lips. He watched as a single tear crested her cheek, which wasn't nearly as red as his own, and continued down her neck, eventually being concealed amid the confines of her modest undersuit.

In the cell, Orion massaged his jaw. It ached with remembrance. The pain brought him, slowly but steadily, back to the present. He was no longer a teenager assigned to a freighter bound for the outer rim. He was an adult—a slightly overweight, renegade Union researcher who had helped the most notorious woman (next to Sonja Lewin, that is) in the solar system evade Union imprisonment.

He smiled. When he thought about what he'd done, his heart no longer sank.

Reality, though, has a frigid and unbiased way of hurling you back into the here and now. And reality said that he was a prisoner, along with Carla and this didactic Silvagno, on a Rover transport.

Ori was tired and hungry. He didn't have the energy to scale the dark wall and make his way to the vine-like path overhead so he could try and kick out the freshly welded grate. And, as he found out moments later, all of that was quite all right.

The door unlatched once again. A pair of eyes, bobbing in the still limited light, entered the cell. Binders clattered to the floor.

"Take these," the invisible intruder said gruffly.

"Bind them first, and then yourself."

Dr. Silvagno felt for the plastic ties and did as he was told. He placed the restraints around Orion's overlapping wrists, trying to keep them as loose as possible. The Rover that had remained silent pushed through the entryway and shoved Eugene aside, yanking on the clasp of the restraints. Ori grimaced as the hair on his wrists, now violently caught by the sharp cuffs, was uprooted.

Soon they were marching toward the bridge of the ship. The stench persisted; in fact, it grew increasingly potent as they reached the end of the hall and first glimpsed the elongated viewing window.

Light. Thank God.

Even though it was faint—a muffled mauve that barely prompted pupil dilation—it was still light. Ori was amazed at how he had taken such a necessary thing for granted. He was sure the quietly glittering control room, under any other circumstances, would likely border on impenetrable blackness. But now he found himself feebly squinting, his eyes being just acclimated enough to the absence of concentrated luminescence to afford him perception.

Rovers moved about the bridge with precision. There wasn't any of the careless, borderline handicapped lumbering he had previously witnessed. Cable paths, now easily visible overhead, converged seamlessly (via what appeared to be graphite bars that jutted out in a rib like arrangement along the walls) with elaborate corridors that traversed the diamond corrugated floor. Like wasps constructing a nest, the Rovers swarmed from one narrow hole to the next, weaving in and out of the various compartments with purpose.

The hybrid brood tended to flashing panels and revolving sim-vids displayed by muted projectors. Orion hated to admit it, but he was impressed. It was much more efficiently constructed than any Union Command Center he had ever encountered.

Fralin came bounding down one of the paths that wove its way across the broad floor, his knuckles drumming against the cold surface as he moved. He came to a heavy stop in front of them. The plume of blonde hair that flamed from his chest pulsed with each breath.

"One of you, I'm assuming, has had some sort of schooling; at least a partial education at the University."

Ori felt his eyes reflexively dart toward the doctor. He hadn't meant to betray the stranger, this oddly blunt scientist who was of a social class Orion knew nothing about.

But that's exactly what he'd done. The Rovers at Dr. Silvagno's sides' caught the indication and one of them unholstered a hefty weapon. The creature buried the muzzle in the small of Eugene's back.

"I'm a doctor," he responded.

"A doctor of philosophy, no doubt," Fralin said, his voice cracking. He cackled nervously at the unexpectedly high-pitched tone. This scared Orion; the hybrid leader was on edge, and, shockingly, displayed some modicum of fear.

"It was evident by your voice. The way you spoke when we first met. You're entirely too proper.

"Unfortunately, I don't have the benefit of the physics and star-mapping classes that a human, such as you, is afforded."

Fralin motioned for the two guards to move them closer to the viewing window. As they continued awkwardly down a path to their left, Fralin barked orders at a young male who sat punching commands into a screen. The technician nodded and manipulated a flurry of levers. His eyes were fixed on Eugene.

"Tell me," he said in a suddenly more serious tone than any of them had expected. "What star is this?"

The doctor approached the flickering map and asked the technician to plot specific nebulae. They illuminated blue and Eugene snatched up a measuring device. He pinched his chin and shook his head emphatically.

"This is wrong. Something's wrong with your scopes. This information is incredibly outdated."

"That was our assessment as well. Apparently, though, diagnostics report no malfunction."

Eugene laughed involuntarily.

"No," he finally said, lowering his head. "It's impossible."

"Is it?" Fralin asked, his yellow canines revealing themselves with mock ferocity.

"Unsheathe the viewing window."

The innards of the room squealed, and the dark shutters retreated into the walls. A piercing yellow disc hovered before them. It was infinitely bright, and, it seemed, incredibly miniscule.

Fralin turned and asked, with tired repetition, "Tell me, doctor, what star is this?"

The Rovers had asked the wrong person to identify the mysterious star. Orion knew, after countless hours spent scrutinizing sim-vids and pouring over his limited collection of historical discs, that it was, without a doubt, the life-giving dynamo that humanity had so cruelly hurled into premature extinction. Only it was tiny and incredibly radiant.

It was an impossibility.

It was the pre-Expansion Sun.

Chapter 15

Sonja awoke face down on the floor of her transport. The panels above her, which spun like neon looms, were almost angelic in the midst of the overwhelming luminosity that coated the interior of her vessel.

She tried to look toward it; tried to identify the unexplained brilliance.

"Solar tint," she commanded in a throaty tone.

Her transport's CPU whirred and buzzed; gears interlocked noisily and her viewing window was concealed, rather loudly, by the convergence of two dark, translucent panes of plexifab. The blinding orange that had swathed the transport was immediately reduced to a gentle golden hue.

She turned over on one side and slowly pulled herself up and into the pilot's chair that was clamped firmly before the nav-system computer robotically babbling coordinates.

The metal plaque she had used to bake the Twilight was overturned on the floor, the remainder of the drug that she hadn't consumed congealed in a half-dollar puddle underneath. Sonja realized the drug had almost completely worn off. It usually took six to seven hours for the after effects to have subsided, but her brain, though slightly hindered by a passive headache, seemed to be in good working order.

"First things first," she said to the stale air. "Where the hell am I?"

She stared at the pulsating display above her nav-system and asked it to identify her location. The floating image flashed briefly before a small diagram of the red sun appeared at the center of the model.

"WARNING," it said sternly, "The ship has entered Expansion space. Reverse course plotted for Neptune Complex."

Sonja looked intently through the viewing window. She saw a bright star, obviously not the Sun, oscillating noiselessly in what had to be some exotic corner of the galaxy. Sonja shielded her brow when the iridescent purples and blues intensified the throbbing in her temples.

"Reconfigure," she said in an irritated voice. The computer's cooling fan began spinning. *These old computers*, she thought morosely, *they're going to end up killing us all.*

"WARNING," it repeated, "The ship has entered—"

"Fine," she hammered the cancel button above the warning beacon. "Fine. Just shut-up, you piece of shit." She raised one of her slender legs and kicked the base of the computer harder than she'd intended. The apathetic voice faltered momentarily and then resumed its emergency message.

Engaging manual operation, Sonja oriented the ship so that its back was turned to the star.

She was frightened. The nearest star was light years away, which meant she was, to put it mildly, in extraordinarily dire straits. She called on everything she had learned at the University on Io—all of the knowledge that she had previously discarded as all but useless—to try and figure out what was going on.

Despite the fact that she was a Twilight addict and an F.P.U. Board member— *the* Board member—she was also a scientist.

In fact, more than *anything* she was a scientist. It was inborn, and, no matter how hard she tried, it was impossible to ignore.

Sonja tried her best to clear her head. It helped that the viewing window allowed her to gaze upon otherwise benign stellar bodies. She was familiar with these intangibles. They were comfortable—in a somewhat abstract way, she found them soothing.

Counting aloud by way of pointedly extending each of her fingers, Sonja sorted through what she knew.

Fact number one: she passed out and felt unusually more nauseous than normal in the minutes following consumption. She vividly remembered her entire body feeling as if it had been stretched. More than stretched; heated—superheated—and then stirred like warm cream. Sonja felt as if she had become malleable to the point of no longer existing as a solid.

Fact number two: pain. Immense, indescribable pain. Though brief, it had been incredibly real. She remembered trying to scream, her vocal cords rattling soundlessly.

Fact number three: the sobering realization that she was on the verge of overdose. There wasn't much documentation on what that was like, as many that finally did O.D., it was presumed, were silently cast off into the region beyond the heliosphere. When they lost control; drifted helplessly in makeshift transports past Pangea, there was no chance of return.

Fact number four: the failed Borsen experiment.

Realization nested in the hollow of her skull.

"No," she murmured. "This was more than a bad trip. This was something else. It's all too...concrete."

Fact number five: her transport's nav-system told her repeatedly that she had entered Expansion space: the "Dead Zone," as it was often called. If that were true, then the name should live up to itself; she should, by all accounts, be a crispy critter. But she wasn't. Sonja was alive and well. All of the idiosyncrasies that had existed prior to her Twilight consumption were still in plain sight, too. The plaque she had so hastily snatched from the wall; the undersuit she had changed into, rather reluctantly, as to have adequate warmth for the journey ahead. Sonja thought about her blue jeans; how she wished she had stuffed them into her ridiculous duffel bag. Now, more than ever, they would've bought an added sense of "right."

More memories, with the force of a gathering tsunami, towered over her, threatening to crest at any moment. She slid out of her chair and onto the cold floor. The engines below idled dully, producing just enough white noise to give her subconscious the time it needed to finally coagulate and press on.

Fact number six: she had left to find Eugene. Sonja had fled the Complex to chase after a stolen transport. She remembered, too, that she had left in a stupor; the Twilight had motivated her to rocket back to the rapidly disappearing blue planet in an effort to capture the 491 pioneer and bring him to justice.

Or was there more to it than that?

The foaming aftermath of her mental typhoon began to recede, and more was revealed about her situation.

The black hole.

Had the Borsen engine actually *worked*?

She scrambled to the darkened viewing window and looked out. There was nothing but the continuous wink of faraway stars.

Seizing the controls, Sonja spun the ship in a slow circle, looking in every direction and checking the nav-system's reports anxiously. She was nowhere near Neptune. The gas giant should've still been visible on her scopes as a hazy crystal ball. It was nowhere to be found. Then, some 26 A.U.s away, her transport detected an alien cloud of rushing gas that seemed to materialize out of nothing.

The same thoughts that had taken control of the man she'd abandoned civilization for wrapped their icy hands around her cerebral cortex.

Had she been consumed by a singularity? It was an impossibility to be sure, but she didn't see any other option. Perhaps, she thought with morose delight, I *did* O.D. And I've been drifting for days. Weeks. Months.

No, she realized sickeningly; *I would have died of dehydration*. Besides, you don't wake up from a Twilight overdose. Despite the lack of documented evidence on the matter, it was common knowledge.

And where did this uncharted star come from?

On the verge of tears, Sonja fought, with her limited strength, to keep panic at bay.

"Madame," her nav-system chimed in politely. "I have a ship in range. Class: UNIDENTIFIABLE."

Sonja was overcome with a strange concoction of shock and joy. She climbed back into the chair and punched commands into the nav-system panel. The tiny image of a craft, with markings she had never seen, was layered into existence on the sim-vid display.

Before she could ask the computer to locate it, the sterile voice continued.

"The vessel is moving deeper into Expansion space." She came to the conclusion that her nav-system charts had been fried.

"Follow it, for Christ's sake!" she shouted excitedly.

The transport's engines thrummed, and soon she was moving at maximum velocity toward the unimaginably bright star.

Chapter 16

Eugene was given a vid-system—which was placed in the center of a desk—and a stiff, metal chair to occupy as he tried to work it all out. After a dizzying cacophony that involved sheered wires and sparking circuitry, the Ark's nav-system had undergone an impromptu reprogramming and was able to reliably decrypt Union signals. The doctor was then able to pinpoint a single contact.

The Borsen engine.

The next hour was spent sifting through the experimental craft's transponder data. The doctor was curled over the vid-system like a fetus. After about thirty minutes, he calmly laid his stylus on the tarnished surface of the workstation.

"It's true," he said, trying to suppress a disturbingly amused smirk. "The engine worked. But the formula they installed to calculate the astronomical units, it seems, interpreted the data in an unexpected way. Instead of punching a hole straight through to 491, the ship entered a prolonged stasis because of the nature of the singularity. A parabola was created; one that measured the weight of the continuum in density according to *years*—not distance."

The Rovers, slouched like gorillas, seemed unimpressed.

"If I'm understanding this correctly," Fralin broke in, "You're suggesting that we…"

"Yes," Eugene finished his sentence. "As insane as it sounds, we breached the theoretical temporal barrier. We time traveled."

Several of the hybrids stammered back against a bank of servers.

Fralin lingered on the far side of the bridge. His bowed arms straightened when he planted them firmly against the floor like crutches. He shot disapproving glances toward Eugene as his fingers moved across a nearby console's display, pulling and analyzing data about the life expectancy of stars and the accepted theories surrounding black holes.

Fralin suddenly swung toward Dr. Silvagno in wide, pendulum-like movements. His eyes were narrow when he began his interrogation.

"What, exactly, have you discovered?" he demanded.

"Just what I've already said. That this star is, without a doubt, the Sun." He felt like a moron when he said it, and his shoulders shrugged involuntarily.

"The Sun. That's what you've come up with?"

"Oddly enough, what our friend Orion here said earlier is entirely correct."

The two guards on either side of Ori released deep sighs. The one on his left looked like he wanted to tear the overweight researcher in two.

"The color," he said, gesturing toward a sim-vid that revolved idly, "Is unmistakable. I checked it against the records four times. And the size," he said, his voice making its transition to lecture mode, "Is wholly unique and we have precise measurements. 1.9891×10^{30} kg. There's no mistaking that."

Fralin moved closer and seemed to stare at the crosshatching of scars on Eugene's hands.

Dr. Silvango leaned back in his chair and casually interlaced his fingers behind his head. Drawing in a deep breath, the doctor then propped his feet up on the desk and retold his story. He cut out a lot of what he considered "unnecessary" details—

Gushkewau'; the odd, tangled ivy that blanketed the surface of the distant planet; the frenzied escape. He spoke in abrupt sentences, and finally ended with his observation of Neptune's fate.

"So you see," he concluded, "The planet is being consumed by a science experiment gone wrong. It's a tragedy. It really is. But one I think we've all heard before."

Eugene laughed at his own joke. No one else did.

Then the doctor had a revelation.

"In fact," he said excitedly, "It should be *here*. *Now*. At least the start of it."

He ordered several technicians to make adjustments. They looked to Fralin for approval; he gave them a comically grave nod.

Sure enough, their scopes detected an unknown nebula coalescing at the former Headquarters location.

Fralin's brow furrowed, the gray, wispy hair that sprung like whiskers from his jawline being smoothed by sausage fingers. He closed his eyes and pinched the apex of his snout. Several Rovers, apparently of higher rank than the guards that presently kept watch over the only humans on board, approached their leader. They instantly backed away upon seeing his meditative posture. They waited silently for him to emerge from his trance.

"If this is true," he finally said, "Then that means..."

"Yes," Dr. Silvango said carefully. "Yes."

"Where are we now?"

"Nearing Jupiter."

He sat up and crossed his arms.

"*When* are we?"

Dr. Silvango cracked his fingers and moved them with accuracy across the vid-system's screen.

The doctor breathed heavily. "39,764 BCE."

"BCE?" Carla mused.

"Before the Common Era. It's an ancient historical designation related to the arrival of the Christian God."

"So what, exactly, does that mean?"

"It means we're at the beginning," the doctor blurted.

"The beginning of what?"

Eugene scanned the bridge with a newly rooted sense of wonder elongating his features.

"The beginning of Man—modern Man. *Civilization*."

Eugene touched the screen and the rotating hologram vanished and was replaced by a condensed diagram of the solar system. A cursor blinked rapidly inside Expansion space. Eugene manipulated several icons.

Suddenly, the bloated Sun was reduced to an ominous blip. Where the cursor had before blinked was now a blue pixel.

Fralin leapt and was soon careening along the tangle of wires overhead. He shouted orders at the stunned hybrids. The Ark's anatomy groaned, and an audible shudder permeated the floor. Orion shifted uneasily in his restraints.

At the center of the pentagonal control room an image descended. It materialized slowly, the pure white at its ends generating a digital aurora in the air just above the hologram.

"This is *live*," Fralin bellowed from his position on the other side of a concealed hall.

A jigsaw segment appeared, like a swollen thumb, pointing south toward a greenish brown continent. The familiar boot, mercilessly kicking the distended Mediterranean, was the tell-tale sign.

"Earth," Fralin whispered in the unshakable stillness. Only a handful of onlookers turned their gaze toward the Commander.

"Earth!" He shouted this time, his voice rising in what ignited a crescendo of triumphant barking.

"Earth! Earth!" he proclaimed repeatedly. Cheers rang from the weary hybrids as they fought to overcome their trademark scoliosis.

As the noise grew, Orion turned to Eugene to try and catch a glimpse of his reaction. He stared at the flickering hologram blankly, his dark eyes the same color as his oily hair.

They had returned to the planet of their forefathers. Their eyes met and it was clear they possessed the same thought; like a snapping arc of electricity, the understanding was mutual.

This was their chance to stop it; their chance to prevent a hellish fate.

"Set course," Fralin said, his voice struggling to regain its military stoutness, "For *Earth*."

Another chorus erupted from the overjoyed Rovers, half of whom dangled giddily from the overhead network, their giant hands slapping the ceiling in rhythmic applause.

Fralin had started lumbering back toward the men, but was intercepted by a Rover that came galloping in from an unseen hatch. He talked hurriedly, his hands moving in sharp, quick bursts.

"They can't find Chiu," Orion mumbled to the doctor.

"Who?" Eugene asked, confused.

"Chiu. She escaped just before you were brought on board. They injected her— "

Orion turned his head to see Orvice being escorted onto the bridge. Ori recognized his eyes. The man's transformation was nearly complete. This was the first time he had gotten a clear look at the creature in the cell next to his own.

He was still mostly bipedal, though his shoulders had been forced into a bone-breaking *V*. His eyes retained the fire Orion had first encountered in the dark, and his mouth had assumed the curled, extended quality that represented such unspeakable ferocity. It wasn't a snout, but it was close. The "man's" nose was covered in perspiration and glimmered in the light of a nearby display.

When the guards stood him next to Orion, the broken form stared at the image of Earth. Ori wrinkled his nose. In the excitement, he had completely forgotten about the smell.

"I see your friend has escaped from her cell," Orvice said absently. "The guards have been stomping about for the past hour. It's been quite the spectacle."

The captive tried to maintain an objective bead on the situation, but it wasn't working.

It was difficult to speak over the incessant howling.

"I hope I don't start sounding like that; at least not for a little while longer."

"I'm sure you won't," Orion said reassuringly. He knew it was a lie, but the researcher felt obligated to try and comfort the metamorphosing animal. Brightening, he turned toward the captive.

"Look," Ori said in his calmest voice, pointing toward the oversized hologram. "It's Earth. I mean, it's *really* Earth. We're going there now. It's not a dream."

"It's not a dream," Orvice repeated absently.

He stared at the sim-vid and spoke again.

"I don't know why they took me out of my cell. I really don't."

Ori didn't say anything.

Without warning, the soon-to-be Rover was doubled over in pain, clutching his neck. Orion spied the injection site. It was like Chiu's: round—perfectly symmetrical. The welt was visible through the thickening fur. A thin line of blood trailed the wound.

The guards ignored him.

"Something's wrong," Eugene croaked.

"What was your first clue?" Ori responded angrily. He turned to one of the Rovers behind them. "He's not taking to his injection. He needs help."

"That happens sometimes," the guard responded in a frustrated tone, an uncaring look momentarily animating his face. "There's not much we can do about it. Sometimes the body adapts; sometimes it doesn't."

Orvice hadn't heard any of the conversation, and Orion was glad. He helped the dilapidated mutation to his feet. Orvice's nose was now running, and long chords of mucus rubber-banded the floor.

The thing sloppily buried his face in a sleeve of his undersuit. He sniffed lustily, then spoke.

"Won't it be nice to actually be *outside*?"

"Yes," he said. "I can't even imagine."

In the corner, beyond where Dr. Silvagno stood repeatedly cracking his knuckles, he saw Carla.

She wept acrimoniously.

Fralin climbed atop one of the center consoles and brandished a ruddy syringe.

"The time has come, my brothers," he declared solemnly, "For us to abandon our artificial form. The time has come for us to go home."

Ori thought about the Beast; the way it had gleaned the steeple of the ice temple.

The way it clung to everything.

Chapter 17

When Fralin ordered the flyby of Mars his crew became impatient. They hobbled around anxiously on battered knuckles, eager to abandon the Ark and taste non-synthetic air.

Centuries earlier Clonpulls had been sent to survey the red planet's northern ice caps, as it was the only region capable of sustaining the multitude of crustaceans which inhabited the environment. Ori had read they were so plentiful that they were eventually transported back to Earth as a culinary delicacy. In Mars-themed restaurants, the super-rich rolled their thumbs across scanners, forking over tens of thousands of dollars. For an extra twenty, the animal would be served alive. It was presented in a plexifab terrarium filled with a block of Martian ice.

When they were discovered it was a big deal. On the television, a white-haired scientist of some kind held a plain white tray. He smiled at the camera, his eyes curving up under the brim of a teal scrub cap. The sim-vid zoomed in on the animal's gray, conical shell and the twelve rigid appendages that hung from its bulk like talons.

Fralin assigned a group of twelve Rovers to leave the Ark on secondary transports. They were to bring back several bushels of the exotic food for consumption during the landing feast.

The crew, however, exhibited a hitherto unseen opposition to the Captain's demands. They protested, branding the task an unnecessary risk.

What if the transports malfunctioned and they couldn't break the planet's gravity? What if the ice wasn't, in fact, as durable as the sim-vids claimed? Earth, they argued, would have an overabundance of sustenance. With their eyes shining and their voices low, they persuaded their leader to conduct a survey of the planet—something to make sure the scholar hadn't lied to them. Something to prove they were really in their own solar system.

Fralin consented. Eugene saw the way he purposely strode by the still spinning sim-vid of Earth on stunted legs; the way he stared at it, salivating—dreaming. He was an officer, but the hybrid couldn't conceal the fact that he was just as anxious as everyone else.

When the probes returned and the nav-system verified that the atmospheric composition was an identical match of the historical records, Fralin was satisfied. The ship plugged along smoothly, its nav-system periodically announcing the time till crossing the threshold into Earth space.

Orion had retrieved Carla from her corner with the permission of the guards. He knelt beside her, one arm wrapped snugly around her torso, whispering something urgent.

Dr. Silvagno realized that, until they landed, he couldn't be absolutely sure of what time period they occupied. It was highly unlikely that the information he'd received was inaccurate, but there was the possibility that the engine misfired—it could have transmitted faulty data. The only way to know for sure was to set foot on the planet.

He also tried to work out his escape plan. Ori would have to help him; he was sure of that. Eugene was smart, but intelligence alone wouldn't be enough to overcome hundreds of rabid Rovers.

"Earth space visible on scope," the nav-system announced loudly. "Moon in range."

In the never-ending discussions about the old world, the only real planet, the Moon was so often neglected. But what a marvelous entity it was; a brilliant rock that, among thousands of other things, kept the oceans in check. What it must've looked like stamped against the stationary stars of a non-polluted world.

"The Sea of Tranquility," Ori murmured.

He had always thought that was the best name for a feature famous for its characteristic serenity. It rolled off of his tongue with ease, and, when he found himself bored, he would often pop in one of many sim-vids that contained detailed surveys of the charcoal feature that cast an eerie luminescence.

Then, through the viewing window, the satellite itself was in range.

The sim-vids hadn't done it justice.

A large portion was covered in shadow, but the crescent sliver that was visible cast another net of silence over the ship. Dotted with craters, it emerged from a cluster of stars as a venerable guardian. Its scars were plentiful and punctuated, marking the demise of countless asteroids that had tried to break through its post and disrupt the sanctuary of Man.

When they were almost on top of it, the talcum surface sprang open in the sunlight, like a sheet on a line being snapped by an unexpected gust. A sprawling landscape of white, settled powder rolled beneath the plexifab window.

Dr. Silvagno noticed it immediately. There were no colonies. At its peak, settlements covered the Moon in artificial light. At night it transformed from a heavenly city into something sinister, the plains flashing scarlet under the proximity beacons of thousands of construction vessels.

Suddenly, over the lengthening horizon, what they had all longed for.

Home.

It appeared first as a discolored halo, the haze of the atmosphere obscuring it from their straining eyes. Then, almost magically, it emerged in the shifting vid-system light.

The seas were a heavy blue verging on black. North America shifted from soft greens to sandpaper browns, the forest giving way to the scrub of vast desert.

"Look," Dr. Silvagno said, pointing toward what most of them recognized as the Floridian peninsula.

"A hurricane."

From several hundred thousand miles away it looked like a harmless, slightly lopsided wisp of cloud that could be extinguished with a deep breath. The reality, of course, was much different. Eugene spoke to Fralin and explained to him that landing there would be insane.

The leader of the Ark seemed to heed the doctor's advice. He called for the vid-system to begin its bio scan. The flat computer wheezed when it sprang into action. Receivers on the hull realigned themselves noisily, and the holo-screen in the middle of the room highlighted the areas with the most life. No one was shocked to see that the entire globe was covered in florescent yellow.

"No," Eugene said calmly. "Search for monumental architecture; buildings."

The computer surged once more, its panel causing a green tint to paint a far wall of the bridge. A small group of Rovers peered through cables and overlapping holograms that shot out above the nav-system computers.

Nothing. The globe spun as it had earlier, not a single piece of noteworthy construction in sight.

Dr. Silvagno cracked his knuckles again and paced nervously.

"Ask it to search for basic settlements."

"Why?" Fralin demanded curtly.

"I have to confirm the year. Please."

Fralin turned away from the dark-haired scientist and moved toward the bio scan computer at a surprising pace. He whispered something to the Rover operating it and gave a this-is-your-last-favor nod to the doctor.

The computer buzzed again and then, in small, bright, tightly compacted groups, the globe was punctuated by light.

"Yes," Eugene said, gnawing gently on the extended pinky of his left hand. "Yes. Okay. France. You see that group of dots?" he asked, pointing to the western European coastline.

"That's where we want to land."

"Why there?"

"Because," Eugene continued, "Those are villages."

"And who says we're trying to find *people*?" Fralin responded gruffly.

Dr. Silvagno lowered his gaze and kept his eyes focused on the toes of his boots.

"If we land on the outskirts, they won't see us. We'll at least have ironclad confirmation of the time period."

Fralin swayed gently. The subtle rocking of his bulky torso made him look like a contortionist that was on the verge of performing some kind of bone-breaking maneuver.

"All right, doctor. I'll grant you this request. Now you are done with demands."

"Nav-system!" Fralin roared.

"Yes, Captain?" it answered, the synthetic voice muddled by a layer of barely audible static.

"Land us at the cluster reference in quadrant IH-9."

"Copy."

With that, Earth vanished behind the lead shield that quickly enclosed the viewing window. The Rovers snapped out of their daze, each one scrambling to his assigned position. Many of them began locking themselves in the ceiling harnesses.

"Secure them," Fralin said to the Rovers that stood watch over the trio at the rear of the bridge.

Carla didn't protest as she was tightly clamped to a restraint that jutted from a nearby wall. Soon, all three of them were standing on tiptoes, the majority of their bodies secured with a series of belts that almost halted circulation.

"Soon we will be in the atmosphere. If the sim-vids are accurate, it will be a shaky descent. But don't look so upset, humans!" Fralin bellowed in a jovial tone.

"In less than an hour, you will be walking the land of your forefathers."

Orion shut his eyes.   The boosters under him groaned and the craft rattled with intensity. For a few seconds, the artificial gravity drive deactivated and he felt what little hair he had lift off of his forehead and effortlessly curl toward his scalp.

The gravity returned almost as soon as it had vanished. But now it was heavier; more defined.

He felt like a grunting weight in the harness, and his groin was abruptly crushed by one of the thin belts. Orion contained his yelp of pain, his eyes and lips trembling, straining to remain closed.

"Walk the land of your forefathers."

He repeated this numbly as the rising roar of flames scorched the Ark's exterior.

Orion pictured the hurricane that was consuming the humid area that would one day be "Miami." He liked the sim-vids he had seen of that city. It was vibrant— wet with color.

Then he remembered the Beast. The way it plowed, without pity or remorse, through the poisonous Jovian soup. He thought of the way it had stared at him day after day while he monitored the infrared scopes.

This new storm, here on Earth, would not be able to look at him. *It will try*, he thought, *but it won't be able to. I'll be too close.*

The rockets died and there was silence.

Then the reverse thrusters fired in twos, leveling their descent. The heels of Ori's feet felt as if they would puncture the floor.

Then there was the winding quiet of the giant mechanism as it finally came to rest.

Chapter 18

Sonja strained to see through the tinted plexifab of her visor. A ray of light that shone through the thick porthole was made cloudy by the rising dust kicked up in the suction of decompression.

The door slid open with the unease of a window that had been painted shut years earlier. It whined and ripped at its seal before finally giving way.

Eternal light. Sonja shielded her face with a gloved hand and thought briefly that she had looked into the face of God. She screeched and stumbled backward. Her rear was involuntarily planted like a sack of charcoal on the flat ramp leading away from the transport.

Her headache intensified, and every time she dared peer through the narrow slit between her fingers it was as if her eyes had undergone corrective surgery by way of blowtorch.

Eventually, though, she overcame the grandeur. Her pupils tightened into pinpricks.

A rocky slope dominated the horizon. It was dotted with thin patches of grass that spread east across an outcropping interrupted by apple-shaped boulders.

Then there was the turquoise sky. Stringy clouds that looked like divine tire tracks hung motionless over distant peaks.

Her boots crunched loudly against the pebbles underfoot. She knelt and ran her hand through them; when they scattered, she delighted childishly at the formation of her very own mini-crater.

Suddenly something fluttered to the ground. Its head was tilted, and its two solid, black eyes appeared indifferent. Then came the song.

It was startlingly melodious and raised goose bumps along the backs of her arms.

A bird.

The conical beak and swiveling head—it was a perfect match to the "Anatomy of a Flying Organism" sim-vids she had studied during her junior year at the University. The animal preened for a moment and then reassumed its totemic posture. A smattering of gray covered its chest, and when its wings were folded dutifully at its sides, all else was a flawless white.

Sonja extended one arm, gently rubbing her thumb and index fingers together.

It stopped moving.

The disoriented F.P.U. Board member held her breath and took one step forward. With a shrill chirp the bird flapped loudly and was airborne, flying low along the plateau ironing out the hillside.

Sonja righted herself and took a deep breath.

There was no mistaking it. This was Earth.

The Union had actually gotten something right, even if by accident; the result of some gross miscalculation. She considered the possibilities; tried to understand how this *was* possible. Unable to suppress the swelling emotions, Sonja jerked at the clamps on her helmet.

She hadn't tested the oxygen content, atmospheric composition or toxicity. The bird, she concluded, was proof enough.

With several clicks and a simmering hiss, the bulky helmet was removed. Sonja's red hair blew forward, along her profile, in the presence of breeze. She exhaled loudly and surprised herself by laughing.

Then she wept.

Once she had removed her gloves and regained her composure, she turned toward the sound of the white bird perched at the top of the slope. The thing released its primitive cry once more, stretched its dramatic wings, and let the wind carry it out of sight.

Without remembering to seal the door to her transport, Sonja began climbing the loose rocks of the hillside. She clawed her way up the tumbling incline, leaving a small avalanche of granulated debris in her wake.

Soon she was at the top, the ground beneath her firm and compact. She tested it with one foot to reassure herself that she didn't have to remain on all fours.

Mountains lined the horizon like jagged teeth chewing at the sky, which had become almost sickly with the arrival of an overcast pallor.

Suddenly a sense of disappointment settled on the exhausted politician.

The Earth was a rock. Granted, she had seen *life*—complex life that she'd previously only dreamed of—in its natural environment, obviously surviving with ease. This wasn't a giant worm pulsating beneath a frozen sky. Still, it was only a bird, and she found this unsettling. The word "gull" lingered in her mind's eye.

Where was the land of milk and honey?

Was this place that much different than Mars? Or even Pluto? She wasn't sure. It had breathable air, a luxury that she had never expected to find on even the most exotic planetesimal during her lifetime. She knew she should be grateful, and in those first overwhelming moments outside of the transport, she had been. She should still be on her knees, she thought, balling, kissing the ground and—perhaps—praising almighty Scuttlebug for His merciful deliverance. But an uncontrollable rage seized her throat and Sonja had the distinct feeling that she'd been duped.

It was a feeling she desperately tried to suppress. Her hands shook. She couldn't have what she wanted.

Was she really that simple? Was she *really* the power-hungry, ruthless-bitch-of-a-Union-official that so many of her subordinates jawed about around the proverbial water-cooler?

Yes. She was. She knew that. The realization smothered her like a wool blanket, shielding her from logic, reason and cold, hard truth. Of course, it also locked in warmth; an unidentifiable heat that soon metabolized into an unquenchable inferno that singed all two billion of her capillaries.

Quietly, with every muscle in her body taught, vibrating with tension, she collapsed to the rocky surface of old.

Pain.

The knowledge that she was no better off now (in fact, by all accounts she was actually in a more desperate situation) than she was at the Complex had settled stiffly into her brain. Sonja imagined that it had found a nice, quiet corner where it could set up base camp so as to go about its business of methodically driving her insane. With all of her strength she tried to reach this intangible, hiding in its veiled corner.

But it was too late.

She knew she would die here, alone.

Then she remembered the ship her nav-system had identified at the edge of Neptune space.

In her excitement, Sonja had allowed her emotions to temporarily take control. But now she remembered. She had come to this particular site to find out where that ship was from. She had come here, in fact, so she would *not* be alone.

With one hand cupped over her brow, she once again surveyed the terrain stretching out before her. Two more gulls—*yes, that's it*—had landed on the rocks below, but it was otherwise a barren environment. A whipping squall caused her vaccusuit to dig its boots into the molehill she now ruled, and the two gulls below took off. She followed them as if they were otherworldly kites that promised some divine revelation. Their wings were motionless as the wind swept them along.

Then she saw it.

A thin trail of dark smoke rose from beyond the teeth.

*   *   *

Carla didn't want to be the first to exit the Ark, but she realized she didn't have a choice. After solemnly receiving their injections of the mysterious orange cocktail, the Rovers surrounded her. Fralin looked much too serious.

"Carla Grayson," he said in a low voice. "You will be the first one to set foot on Earth. Do you find this ironic?"

She didn't say anything.

The Captain barked deeply and motioned to the guards that held Ori and Eugene.

"After the airlock releases, you will follow Carla out onto the surface."

"Why?" Dr. Silvango asked absently.

"We have to test the air. Computers, for all their wonders, are not infallible."

Fralin smiled and licked his lips. The airlock was dark, and the tinted porthole emitted a skewed interpretation of how blinding the outside world would be. The small band of Rovers that was assigned to escort them onto the surface had suited up quickly. They were covered in thick fabric and dark helmets.

The anxious hybrids hobbled over to the prisoners and pushed them forward.

Dr. Silvagno whispered to his companions.

"When the lock opens, we're going to have to make a run for it."

Neither Orion or Carla looked up, but their shifting eyes told him they were listening. The doctor coughed loudly and cleared his throat. Fralin and his commanding officers were approaching.

"Just trust me," he said. "They think they know how bright it will be, but they don't. Their eyes won't be able to take it... even with the visors."

Ori gave a slight nod and glanced toward Carla to see if she had heard. She stared at the two men and shrugged her bony shoulders.

"You are pioneers," Fralin said. "Now lift your heads and be proud. We're making history."

The door behind them closed and an ominous *clang* rang from the spinning latch in front of them.

One of the Rovers behind them grunted and spoke in a gruff voice.

"Don't try anything, or we'll be forced to kill you."

"What would we try?" Eugene inquired playfully.

He felt the muzzle of a chain gun probe the area between his shoulder blades.

The door opened, and the outside air came rushing in. Without their helmets on, the three were, momentarily, breathless. They gasped loudly and then swallowed the sweet air in gigantic gulps. It was alive.

They were so absorbed in the moment that they didn't initially perceive the sunlight. It was, as the doctor had indicated, blinding. The three humans turned their heads toward the Rovers and shielded their eyes.

With short stabbing motions, they were prodded away from the vessel and into a scorched clearing. The trio emerged from the shady airlock of the ship cautiously, their steps short and calculated.

It looked like Carla's eyes were completely shut, the skin at the corners constricted in a fan of wrinkles. Dr. Silvagno saw that they were partially open, though, and his own eventually made contact with the thin slits of white and blue that were barely perceivable.

She smiled weakly and nodded.

They were off.

Their feet stamping in synch, weightily and like pistons, they ran awkwardly across the undulating terrain. Carla had forgotten the degree to which an undersuit could weigh a person down when in the presence of considerable gravity—it wasn't as bad as a vaccusuit, but it was no picnic.

Orion caught up with them quickly. He wanted to deliver a stern slap to the back of Eugene's head for giving the signal without considering his position. Thankfully, the researcher had been cognizant enough to hear their feet shuffle before the Rovers knew what was happening.

Dr. Silvagno looked over his shoulder and saw the wavy silhouette of a Rover wallowing on the ground. Two others exited the Ark and dragged him into the bowels of the ship.

"What did I tell you?" he asked between panting breaths. "They can't take it. Even with the visors."

"Yeah, you're a genius," Ori shouted, his gut heaving with every colossal step. "Now what the hell are we supposed to do?"

Eugene hadn't planned that far ahead. Typically, he wasn't a spur-of-the-moment kind of guy, but his instinct told him that they needed to ditch the Rovers, pronto. As the doctor's eyes adjusted to the piercing light, he weighed their options. He couldn't see everything in front of him, and he stumbled frequently, like an elephant trying to maneuver through a tightly packed tire training obstacle course. But he could see the ground more clearly now, and was able to plant each successive footfall with just enough accuracy to gain valuable traction.

Dr. Silvango looked back once more and saw that the Rover transport had grown small amid the heavy boulders—it was now little more than a bulky piece of tin glinting in the unbearable glow of the Sun. They all stopped abruptly and allowed themselves time to recover.

Ori's face glistened, clean lines of sweat trickling from underneath his thin mat of hair.

"We need to find some sort of cover," he said impatiently. "They'll come after us."

"I don't think so—not yet, anyway. They'll wait 'til dark."

Carla raised one of her pale hands and wiped away a heavy bead of perspiration that had gathered between her nose and her upper lip.

Tenderly, she massaged the back of her neck. It stung and felt like it had been severely burned in the few minutes they had spent sprinting across the wasteland.

"Look!" Ori blurted in a voice much louder than he'd intended. "There's something there... over there, on the other side of that hill."

Orange flames, surrounded by flickering bands of heat, licked greedily at a pile of broken tree limbs some two hundred yards away. It was a small arraignment; something organized. A thick column of black smoke rose from the soil, and they all noticed that the ground ahead of them leveled out and became much more granulated.

Without a word, they picked their way through the loose stones. A cluster of swaying trees drew them in, their giant trunks anchoring rubbery tops that creaked loudly and leaned in the wind.

Ori closed his eyes and let the air brush across his brow; he absorbed the muffled sound it made as it passed over the dish of his ears. When it finally died down, his mind was empty. Then he allowed a single, isolated thought to plop like a lead ball bearing into the depths of his consciousness.

He couldn't predict the patterns of the wind.

It wasn't like the air generators or the seventy-five year-old Schultz converters that still existed in the world he had so abruptly abandoned.

"When it gets dark, they'll come."

Eugene turned drearily to the pair standing behind him.

"And there's no telling what that serum will do."

Chapter 19

The entrance to the cave was shallow.

Dr. Silvagno had spent entirely too much time prodding at the fire outside with a partially blackened stick. He extracted the remains of a small mammal from the ashes—an omen that made Carla nervous. She wrung her hands. Eugene told her to quit being irrational; that this was obviously the domain of a man. "Well, not *definitely* a man," he said with jocular reluctance, "Possibly a woman. But, at the very least, a *person*."

Ori had spent his time lounging in the shade of the enormous trees that created a natural foyer for the cave. Brittle pine needles littered the soil. He had created a makeshift mattress by clumping a group of the brown nettles into a thin pile and then crushing it with awkward CPR motions. Orion had just allowed sleep to sweep over him when Eugene slapped his legs with one of the ashy limbs.

Now the trio stood wearily just inside the low entrance to this rocky hole that partially shielded the dwindling fire from the lulling breeze.

Dr. Silvagno raised his right arm and quietly said, "Lights."

The optic florescent embedded in his sleeve broke the gaping darkness.

The place looked like a hollowed out log. The walls were a deep and rough. Farther back, stalagmites hung like muddy ice sickles from the ceiling. The air was not as fresh as it had been outside; still, it wasn't stagnant. It was wild—similar to the odor they had endured aboard the Ark, but (thankfully) not nearly as pungent. Here, at least, there was a planet's worth of room available for ventilation.

As they moved deeper into the cave, the waning twilight grew faint, eventually dissipating altogether. When they spoke, their voices echoed and vanished into the dark.

"We should leave," Carla said gravely.

"We will. I just want to look a little longer. It's not every day you get to—"

"She's right, doctor," Ori interjected. "This isn't safe. There's no telling what lives here."

"What the hell is wrong with you? Do you think some sort of undomesticated *animal* is able to construct a controlled fire like the one outside? It's not. That was done by a person; nothing else. A person wouldn't share a cave with something else—especially not something dangerous."

Dr. Silvango angled his right arm into the darkness ahead. A hewn wall—which was only just visible—glimmered where water had seeped through its vesicles and trickled down its sheer features.

"I can't believe it." The doctor was mesmerized.

A series of paintings lined the crevices before them, and they were stunningly articulate. One in particular caught Carla's eye.

It was a picture of what appeared to be an elephant, but the skin was a reddish-orange. The silhouette was perfectly rendered. The legs were thin but fashioned with skill; there were indications of stability, strength, simplicity. There were no unnecessary elaborations. The animal's tusks were black, and hung low from its jaw like brooding fishhooks.

"It's an elephant," she said playfully.

"It's not an elephant," Eugene said. "It's a mammoth."

"A what?" Orion asked.

"A mammoth. A wooly mammoth. They died out during the last Ice Age."

"Interesting," Orion replied. "Why would someone paint a mammoth?"

"It was supposed to give them some sort of supernatural power during the hunt. In a way, this was akin to capturing the animal's soul."

"Looking into the Beast," Ori said with a shiver.

"Something like that," the doctor added.

"It's red because it was covered in follicles."

"Ah," Carla said, feigning interest.

"There," Eugene said, his breath slow and steady. "Look *there*."

He shined the blue light from his sleeve toward the floor of the cave, where a pile of worn debris had been neatly fixed in a wide circle. At the edge of the mat was the hollowed out knot of a large branch.

Dr. Silvagno crawled toward the bowl on his hands and knees like he was stalking a jittery gazelle.

"This," he said quietly, "Is a miracle."

Inside the bowl were rounded twigs and stains. Berries that had not yet been ground lay in the bowl, crisp and delicious.

"I don't get it," Carla said. She wrinkled her nose and looked like a ghost in the pale light beaming from the optic florescent.

"This painting is new. Or, rather, it's somewhat new. No older than a few years, if I had to guess. Whoever occupies this cave is a talented artist. During a time like this, it's absolutely amazing."

"A time like this?" Orion asked, annoyed by Eugene's assumption that everyone had been awarded his education.

"This is identical to the paintings found at Chauvet-Pont-d'Arc. When these were found before the first Expansion, they were dated at around 33,000 years old."

Eugene glanced past the group and into the reeling black. He strained his eyes, but saw nothing.

"We should probably leave."

"Thank you," Carla said, a relieved expression smoothing her features.

When the oblong mouth of the cave was in sight, they saw that the sky had become a shady remnant of its earlier self. Then Orion noticed that the fire had been extinguished. White smoke drifted from the ashes in a single gray curl and raindrops pattered against the cinders.

"Damn it," Eugene muttered. "We need to get out of here."

"The storm's already here," Ori said flatly. "Perhaps if we would've left earlier, this could've been avoided."

He stared out of the uneven entrance and thought about the Schultz converter; how its sole purpose had been to extract water from the glassy floes. He thought of how it scurried across the Europan ice, whirring and buzzing, scanning frantically, searching with its shiny tentacle for the liquid so vital to humanity's existence.

Here, such things fell from the sky in abundance.

As the drizzle gave way to a roaring downpour, Ori began, for the first time, to fully understand what mankind had done. He began to have an unobstructed comprehension of what a tragedy this planet, which had sustained his ancestors for countless eons, had waiting for it in the suddenly-not-so-distant future.

Surveying the snuffed out fire barely thirty feet away, he silently acknowledged that this paradise would inevitably be lost. Even if the three of them erected a giant monument of warning that could weather the ages; the floods and the frozen epochs would certainly take their toll. The future *was* set; they were simply playing their predetermined roles in the sprawling drama.

His heart sank.

He stumbled over the uneven ground and stood peering out of the cave.

The smell of the rain was intoxicating. Ori extended his arms and let it spray over him. He let the torrents tease the cave and quilt his face in frigid droplets. A minute later, he retreated into the rocky embrace of this alien dwelling and quietly slurped at the rainwater still leaking from his cupped hands.

He splashed what was left across his chest and inhaled its scent.

For a long time, he didn't say anything. None of them did. Eventually he crawled toward his companions, who were sitting with their backs against a wall. They peered in his direction, but looked past him.

When Ori turned, he saw a dark figure cutting through the rain.

They were petrified—the only sound was the steady beat of the deluge intermingled with the muffled clapping of far-off thunder.

Shadows merged with shadows, and for a moment it all seemed little more than a cruel illusion.

Then, illuminated by the blue bulb of Dr. Silvagno's undersuit, Sonja emerged.

Her hair stuck to her shoulders in matted clumps. The padded soles of her boots sank into the frothy ground. The optic florescent followed her as she approached, and, when she was no more than five feet away, she drew her lips into a narrow smile. Dr. Silvagno switched off his light.

"How... how the hell did you get here?" He stared at her dumbly.

"The same way you did," she said, her voice barely audible against the now pounding thunderbolts.

"You illegally left Headquarters. You stole F.P.U. property."

Eugene laughed.

"Are you kidding? You followed me into a black hole because I stole a one hundred year-old transport?"

Her smile was gone now. She looked past the doctor.

"And what about them?"

"We shared a cell. There were Rovers."

Sonja frowned. "They're here," he said gravely. "Right now."

Orion squirmed. Undoubtedly, she had seen the broadcast. There was—*is*—a steep price on his head (along with both Carla and Chiu, for that matter). "Hell," he thought with growing realization. "She probably authorized the transmission of the damn thing."

"Don't worry," she said, seemingly reading his mind. "I won't turn you in."

Dr. Silvagno chuckled once more.

"Yeah, I believe you won't turn any of us in. Do you have any idea what has happened? Do you know where you are?"

Sonja nodded slowly, the large dose of Twilight she had consumed only hours ago still lingering. Despite her nearly complete recovery Sonja's head throbbed, sometimes in perfect coordination with the deafening peals that tore across the night sky.

She kneaded her temples gently. Sonja shivered—she needed the drug. She needed consumption. Her mind turned to the now smoldering embers that fought for survival. If she could take the snippet she had broken off before she emerged from her ship and heat it up—maybe on a piece of bark—she could guzzle the stuff before it solidified. A real, pure dose.

This would make her rational; ready for thought; ready to outthink Eugene. Her eyes widened and glazed.

She started toward the entrance, but tripped on a finger-shaped rock she couldn't even see. Her palms fell flat against the slick interior.

Carla covered her mouth in the darkness when Sonja vomited. The ruthless leader of the Union was curled up into a tight ball, tens of thousands of years from her own time, her perfectly sculptured sucking in prehistoric air.

Carla imagined that the color had finally returned to her sunken cheeks. She imagined that she appeared "healthy" to others. People no longer cringed or bowed away at her presence. She imagined that the emaciated ribs that concealed and protected her vitals had filled out. She imagined that she had finally taken revenge for six hundred years of injustice.

"Jesus," Ori said, maneuvering across the slick floor to where the weakened leader lay.

"What's wrong with her?"

Eugene looked down at Sonja, a swell of pride causing him to draw in a deep breath of real, non-manufactured air and hold it longer than he had intended. He thought that he should hate himself for relishing the pain she was now stricken with, but he didn't. He loved it.

Dr. Silvango knew about her weakness; her insatiable craving for the narcotic. The consensus was that she had overcome it, but now, witnessing the putrid symptoms only a bona fide addict would display, he knew that wasn't true.

He thought of his failure at the school, how he was left standing like an imbecile over the greasy carcass of the Rover. It was something that had penetrated every pore of his mind—including his dreams. It was a memory that he didn't want Gushkewau' to see, but something it had managed to see anyway.

Gushkewau'.

Even *thinking* its name took more effort than Dr. Silvagno had expected. He knew there was a possibility that it had survived the event horizon.

Eugene instructed Orion to lay Sonja on her back. Dr. Silvagno reached into the belt of his undersuit and extracted a small green tablet. He jammed it into her quivering mouth and pinched her nose. She gasped and clawed at his throat.

Suddenly, her body relaxed. Her breathing slowed and her eyes came into focus. Sonja stared at Eugene and managed a feeble smile.

Moving close to her ear, he whispered, "I need you to be sharp. We can get through this, but not alone. I need you."

She coughed and pulled his head a little closer.

"I know," she said softly.

The rain tapered off, and the thunder became less frequent. Eugene helped Sonja get to her feet.

"We really should get out of here," he said, his eyes turning to Carla.

"Thank you," she mouthed sarcastically across the darkness. They moved out of the cave quickly, their boots splashing quietly in the pool that had formed just inside the entrance. When they emerged the mosquitoes swarmed. Carla swatted at them furiously, crushing several that had perched on the top of her hands, reducing them to bloody streaks.

"I hate these things," she said to Ori as they walked, scratching at the welts that had started to form.

"I don't mind too much," he said almost inaudibly. Carla peered at him in the light of the rising moon. She had only known him for several days, but, in that time, realized that this was the most genuine smile she had seen him produce.

Chapter 20

A symphony of lilting insects overwhelmed them—for a long time, perhaps an hour or more, they did nothing but listen. It was Eugene that had broken the silence.

"On 491, it was different at night. There was no moon. It was black. And when Alpha Centauri had set, there was absolute quiet."

Orion had tuned him out. He had to admit that he was interested in Dr. Silvagno's account of 491, but it could wait. For his entire life, Ori had dreamt of what it would be like to actually set foot on a habitable planet. He postulated and imagined until he was dizzy, but here he was, soaking up the real McCoy. The middle-aged researcher refused to let anything interfere with the experience.

Suddenly the doctor stopped talking. The wet grass rippled in the night breeze and carried with it the sound of snapping twigs. Instinctively, they lowered themselves until they were hugging the ground.

A thin man materialized in the brush. He was dark against the trees, but there was a sense of efficiency in his gait.

The man stopped and tilted his head. He listened. There was a damp thud when he dropped something into a thicket.

No one dared move. Their breathing became shallow as an odd mixture of curiosity and terror electrified their nerves. After several minutes of remaining motionless, the man reached out with one of his bony arms and retrieved his cargo. As he drew close, they were able to see his face bobbing in the moonlight. It was completely enveloped by a tangled beard; his hair was an indistinct bramble that fell to his shoulders; the leftovers of some unknown foliage peppered his cheeks.

He was also completely naked.

The man moved across the clearing quickly. As he strode past the group, they saw that he was dragging an animal. In the pale reflection of the Moon, which was slightly muted by passing clouds, it looked like a small deer. There were a series of white splotches that ran along its abdomen, and its tongue trailed like a dead salmon. It had large, black eyes that appeared fixed on the foursome as it was pulled through the undergrowth. A small row of jutting, yellow teeth mimicked a smile.

They saw, too, that the man was walking with the aid of a long, gnarled branch. Carla was the only one that noticed that it had a sharpened stone fastened to one end. It seemed to prod the sky.

When they could no longer hear the stranger, Eugene spoke up.

"We should follow him," he said curtly.

None of them exhibited anything close to enthusiasm. Carla was the first to respond.

"Did you notice that he was carrying a spear?" Eugene shrugged and looked at the others.

"No, I didn't," he said dryly. "But how do you suppose he killed that thing? By giving it a good talking-to?"

Sonja chuckled.

"Look, if we're going to survive out here, we're going to need to enlist the help of someone who knows this place. None of us know what we're doing; that's for damn sure."

"Yeah," Ori interjected, "But how do we know he won't try to kill us?"

"He won't. Trust me." Dr. Silvagno said this with a forced smile, though Orion's assertion had some credence. There was no telling how this primitive human would react to their presence. Here, it was survival of the fittest. And, by all accounts, he seemed to be just that.

Eugene sighed and provided a brief concession. "You're right, Orion. The man doesn't speak English, or probably any other language we'd recognize. He knows how to hunt, make sharp objects, eat, and reproduce. And that's probably it."

The doctor paused dramatically before continuing.

"Oh yeah, and he knows how to *paint*. So, you see, he does have a sensitive side."

Sonja laughed again, this time much more loudly than she should have. Eugene was quick to clap one of his hands over her mouth and deliver a cutthroat gesture. They sat listening for several minutes, but all they encountered was the same natural song that had occupied the night up until the man's arrival.

"I have an idea," Sonja said, her face visibly turning red by the light of a dimmed optic florescent.

"We need to send a woman." She looked at Carla who withdrew and clutched Ori's arm.

"That's how it works. Remember the course in Early Civilizations?" Eugene rolled his eyes. She smiled at his response.

"It seems to be the most likely way to not startle a man of his—um—social caliber." She removed her jacket and began unzipping her undersuit.

"If we approach him clothed in garments from the 27th century we'll likely be impaled. I didn't get a chance to ask him if he's a 'fight or flight' kind of guy, but I don't think it's worth the risk."

Soon, Sonja was fully exposed. She covered herself with her hands and pulled her knees up to her chest for warmth. "This is the best idea I've got," she concluded in a defeated tone.

Orion had turned away as she undressed. He listened to her speak, and, as insane as it seemed, he believed she was right. This was, in fact, the most logical way to earn the man's trust. Beads of sweat had formed on Carla's forehead. Her eyes fluttered quickly among her companions.

"What's wrong with you," Sonja asked in an irritated tone. "You're not the one going in there."

"I know," she said meekly. "I'm just nervous for you."

Sonja crawled over to where Carla sat. For the first time in years, she felt she was being offered genuine concern from another human being. Tears welled up in her eyes. One managed to escape the cradle of her eyelid and slipped down a freckled cheek. Sonja placed a hand on Carla's shoulder.

"Thank you," she said with more tenderness than Eugene would have ever thought possible.

"Listen," he began again, "Maybe you're right. Maybe this is the best way to approach him. But that doesn't mean it's not dangerous. We'll follow close behind." He started to hand her an optic florescent, but realized she had nowhere to conceal it. "I was going to say that you could use this as a signal." She realized it too, and shivered in the cold night air.

"If anything is wrong, just..." He thought for a second, and was about to speak when she said, "Scream."

"Yes," he said coldly. "Just scream."

Sonja moved through the tangle of milkweed and thorny brush numbly, and, for a moment, forgot she wasn't wearing any clothes.

Then the hunger set in. Her stomach rumbled, but even if she had access to it, she wasn't sure if she could digest any solid food. "Supplements would be good now," she thought, "I could at least keep those down." That was the first time in her life that she had actually preferred rations over actual food.

It was her intention to tell Eugene that a beacon had been detected. She wasn't sure if he had put it all together yet. He seemed to be too taken with the prospect of taking the "hands-off" approach and collecting all of the data he possibly could before making a move. But why? Did he think he could get home?

Home. She whispered the word with emphatic irony.

Sonja knew it was his scientific training—the methods he had learned at the academy had become second nature. She thought of how clumsy he was as a student; how he fought with more ferocity than all of the others to win her affection. It was something that ultimately deterred Sonja. *She* wanted to have to fight for *his* affection. Even at that age, she had grown tired of being able to control everything around her with little-to-no effort. Challenges were good.

When a damp log popped on the nearby fire, her thoughts shifted to the impending confrontation.

She wished she would've stayed clothed. This man, no matter how far removed from any semblance of civilization, would have enough brains to realize that she was, after all, a woman. If he can throw a rudimentary weapon and kill something as agile as an undomesticated deer, then he could certainly bash her over the scalp with a club and proceed as he desired.

More than anything, Sonja wished she still had her undersuit on for the sole purpose of plucking the little piece of glassy plexifab from her breast pocket. If she had the promise of that wonderful iridescent sliver, maybe she could ignite something undomesticated in her own heart and subdue the wild man.

She found herself quivering with desire. Then Sonja focused; remembered why she was here—why she was venturing into this yawning chasm that led into the living Earth.

After all, she was the one that had volunteered to strip down—to become stark naked—because, like her colleague Dr. Silvagno, her inquisitive instincts couldn't be suppressed. In her lower intestine a feeling emerged; a feeling that told her she would die here if necessary. As far as she knew (and as far as anyone else knew), this was the only time in history that a species had been able to actually observe *itself* at the beginning—to probe its own origins.

The urge she had initially felt to inform the others that there was a Union beacon spewing streams of coordinate data only five miles from their current location had all but disappeared. It had taken her the entire length of her walk from her crippled ship to come to the most rational conclusion: the beacon had been activated by the vessel itself, as a fail-safe. Its strength and clarity were too powerful to have come from the ragged transport Eugene had stolen. And, she knew, it couldn't have come from the supply ship the band of marauding mutations had escaped with days earlier on Pluto.

Logic told Sonja it was the Borsen Transporter.

The whole process was like clockwork.

When the nav-system detected a problem with the ship's location, it engaged the "run-home" directive. Simply put, it used its sensors to determine where the densest concentration of human life was and made a beeline accordingly. It was guided by the presence of genetic signatures. In her universe, it would've returned to the Neptune Headquarters. In this universe, it did the only thing it could. The ship landed here, on Earth, possibly (she hypothesized) near the largest gathering of humans on the planet.

That's what made this man they had encountered so odd—as of yet, there had not been any evidence of others. Sonja also realized that the ship was still five miles away. The largest civilization here, in this time, might be no more than a few dozen Homo sapiens sharing an alcove, only having just discovered the full benefits of tools. Concepts like agriculture were still novelties.

"Facing one is better than a dozen," she reported to the night.

The rising wind swept through the pines and brushed against her shoulders. She shook fiercely and exhaled what little warmth she could generate into cupped hands.

When Sonja neared the cave, she saw the deer in the flickering firelight, its stiff legs orange and radiant. The man was nowhere to be found.

Over her shoulder was the outline of her protectors. Their heads were even with the prickly shrubs. A pang of guilt seized her. There was the very real possibility that she was costing these strangers, who had healed her and offered words of encouragement that she didn't deserve, their lives.

From the heart of the cave, an echo; something flat and hard. A *drip drop* followed by silence. The insects continued their chant.

Sonja turned and nodded to her companions. She stood, skirted the fire, and entered the black.

Chapter 21

The pines shivered with the weight of something unseen. It wasn't the wind. Ori was sure of that. And it wasn't just something.

It was some *things*.

Eugene strained to see up and into the trembling branches; the pale leaves continued to rustle under an invisible bulk.

Sonja had been in the cave for over an hour, and, for the most part, there was only silence. It worried them. Dr. Silvagno, possessing the kind of staunch pessimism that could only stem from years of rigorous scientific study at the University, assumed she had been murdered quickly and efficiently.

He had all but forgotten about her when he pinpointed the source of the mysterious noise. A pair of eyes were revealed and hovered in the concealed heights. They were more radiant here, in the muted reflection of the Moon, than they had ever been aboard the sickening confines of the Ark.

More of the shimmering retinas emerged. The forest looked almost festive as the trees took on the holiday twinkle that the doctor had studied the "Religious Celebrations" sim-vid.

Then he remembered that the ancient tradition of Christmas trees carried the very real danger of entirely consuming one's home in flame.

Carla and Ori noticed Eugene's silence, and, when they took sight of the dipping branches, they froze. Dr. Silvagno examined the position of the Moon and realized that hoping for the dawn was a pipe dream. At best they had five (maybe six) hours before the first rays crowned the range to the east. Eugene felt like an idiot—he should've seen this coming. The Rovers would instinctively be skilled trackers; they likely had no trouble identifying which path the escaped prisoners had taken.

The doctor also knew that if they tried to escape they would be overtaken in seconds.

"You shouldn't have run," a voice muttered from above.

Fralin. Eugene singled him out among the others, watching the Rover's eyes narrow as he spoke.

"There's another with you. The Union Board member: Sonja Lewin. Where is she?"

Carla squeezed Dr. Silvagno's arm and shook her head slowly. Several of the Rovers laughed.

"We will kill you. Make no mistake about that. Even if you tell us where she is, you're dead. But we're in a generous mood—seeing as we'll never have to endure an existence in that God-forsaken ship again—so if you tell us where she is now, we'll do it quickly."

Eugene thought about Sonja—how he had known her for a long time. He thought of the way she took pleasure in butterflying the Rover corpse at the academy, and how he had immediately taken her for a selfish, power-hungry dictator-in-waiting. She had, at one time, been very cruel to him. He couldn't forget that. As much as he wanted to tell the panting beasts that now hovered over him that she was no more than a hundred feet away in the depths of the cave, he couldn't.

"No," he said curtly, slowly backing away from them as he delivered his response.

"I guess you'll just have to take your time about it." As he said the words, his blood ran cold. The doctor knew, the very second that they descended, he would endure excruciating agony until his life was swiftly snuffed out at the whim of the insane hybrid commander.

For a moment, an eerie quiet blanketed the landscape.

"Have it your way, human," Fralin retorted, his voice rising as he pushed off of a limb.

The other eyes fell toward them in unison. Then a cry rang out.

Carla jumped, surprised at the intensity and genuine anguish that the tone embodied. The Rovers' eyes searched for their stricken companion, and when he was located, a great wail arose from the group. The three fugitives watched the eyes roll up and into their sockets. Soon, the sickening collapse of flesh and bone against packed dirt. The creatures' cries sounded in rhythmic moans.

Another shriek; this one louder and more intense than the last. The Rovers abruptly retreated into the inky recesses of the wilderness.

When they were gone, Orion stood and approached the patch of earth they had trampled in their panic. He called for Eugene.

"Activate y-your optic f-florescent," he stammered.

Dr. Silvagno switched it on and they peered down at two dead hybrids. One had a long, twisted piece of wood protruding from his chest. When they moved closer, they saw a stone spearhead fastened to the tip of the weapon with tightly wound lashings. Blood ran perpendicular to the shaft in tendril-like globs.

The other Rover lay nearby. Part of his forehead had been crushed. About three feet away was a thick limb that had been cut and planed. Large stones were attached at each end. Blood pooled silently around the Rover's mouth.

Then they noticed the change.

The snout was no longer as pronounced as it had been. In fact, it seemed to have been pulled back tightly by some invisible force. His brow, too, wasn't nearly as steep. The creature was no longer covered in hair, and his legs had elongated.

It was almost human.

"What just happened?" Carla asked, her voice arching in surprise.

"Apparently, someone interceded on our behalf," Dr. Silvagno said. "Unless you made this." He carefully picked up the crude mace.

Carla laughed, which caused her male cohorts to smile. Her giggle was high and child-like, a sound Orion had only heard once before. Seeing only her outline, he thought of how he had wanted to find a way to turn her in when she and Chiu had forced themselves into his hovel. He remembered how she had pressed the gun into the small of his back and forced him to aid in their escape. She seemed so different now with her guard down, her rough exterior stripped away and replaced with a totally personable—totally *human*—demeanor that he had not expected to come from the "Great Orchestrator" of Earth's destruction.

Eugene stepped on a small pinecone, and one of its thorns penetrated a weak spot in the sole of his undersuit.

"Shit!" he screamed, lifting the wounded foot and massaging it tenderly. Ori could see that his face had turned red, and he eventually put his foot down just long enough to field-goal-kick the conifer between a pair of saplings. It spun off with a mild *whiz* into the darkness.

"We should check the cave," he said irritably. "If Lewin's not in there, we'll have to fan out."

"If..." Orion started, but was cut-off by Eugene.

"...she's still alive."

*   *   *

Sonja had entered the cave as nothing more than a silhouette, scarcely highlighted by the moonlight permeating the narrow entrance. The sound she had heard upon her first encounter with the mysterious place continued. A *drip drop* followed by a hard smack. It thrummed.

"Hello?" she said softly, her voice barely carrying an echo against the jutting walls.

Hello, she thought angrily. *As if that'll* mean *anything*.

The sound in the back of the cave stopped.

There was a shuffling of feet, and Sonja believed she could make out the sound of labored breathing. She continued forward, her bare body growing colder in the absence of the summer air she'd known outside.

Once she was no longer visible by moonlight, a subdued grunt resonated. Sonja paused and listened to the eardrum whistle of absolute silence.

She pressed on until she reached a point where she couldn't see anything. Cautiously, she outstretched both arms and waved them in front of her, inching forward as if she'd been blindfolded.

Sonja stumbled over the uneven cave floor, holding her breath as she went. The cool air encircled her body and she began to tremble. Then her hands touched something.

It was the chest of a man. The sprout of hair; the slender, flat pectorals—it startled her, and she yelped. She withdrew her hands and brought them up to her mouth. The man in front of her knelt and pulled her down with one hand. He made a sound she couldn't interpret. She shivered and waited, and the sound came again.

It was a grunt of some kind; something that she wasn't sure could be classified as a word, but it carried a note of curiosity. She tensed, expecting the worst. Sonja knew that any second this proto-human would pounce. For the first time, she felt wholly vulnerable.

She wanted her undersuit. She wanted to be covered; clothed and unexposed. She wanted to have at least *someone* else in there with her. Anyone. Sonja wished she had found a way to melt the Twilight before she had returned to the cave. If she had, then maybe this would all be something different. Maybe this man would be someone she could comprehend; someone she could talk to. There was the real possibility that they would be on a beach sipping mixed drinks and exchanging playful banter about God-knows-what. There would probably be a bucket filled with steamed blue crab and a small, wooden mallet lying between them. They would gorge themselves on the dead crustaceans until they passed out under the yellow Sun.

But that wasn't the situation. She was in what seemed a dark dream, each and every one of her senses true—fully alert. Sonja heard the man back away, and she squinted at the unexpected sight of sparks. A rapid grinding and scraping told her he had a flint.

For a reason she couldn't pin down, this calmed her. She watched the light shower continue, and she managed to discern the man's face during each split-second of illumination. It was dirty and contorted. He was bent over a pile of kindling, his eyes wincing with each stroke of the rough stone.

The dry stuff finally ignited; the flashing combustion seemed to take them both by surprise. The man placed the ball of burning debris into the center of a group of rounded stones. He set the flint aside and stared at Sonja.

She could see that his teeth were crooked and stained. He was missing one of his canines. His beard was knotted and long, and he sat with his grimy knees pulled up to his chin. Sonja tried her best to conceal her disgust at the smell. She wrinkled her nose and tried to breathe through her mouth, hoping to temporarily squelch the overwhelming body odor.

Then she noticed the rudimentary bowl they had seen earlier. It was now filled with a dark paste, and there was a worn stick beside it. The man drew close.

His breathing became erratic and he put one of his hands on her shoulder. She fell back and closed her eyes, shuffling her legs and trying to back away. He immediately stopped.

She peeked through her fingers and saw that he had returned to his original position, crouched next to the bowl of dark liquid. Sonja scrambled back to her feet and did her best to cover herself. The man tilted his head, and she watched his large, brown eyes move in the firelight. After a time, he turned and picked up the bowl.

He sprinkled a variety of berries into it. They plopped noisily. Then, from a container she had not seen, he added a small amount of water. Another drip. He then placed the bowl on the cave floor and picked up the stick. He began jamming it into the bottom of the bowl with hard, hollow smacks.

In amazement, she watched him dip his finger into the bowl and begin creating an image on the cave wall. He started with small, flowing lines that came together in sharp points. Then he worked laterally, adding a smooth curvature and additional lines that plummeted sharply. Sonja realized he was painting the slain deer.

The man worked in silence. Every so often he added dry leaves and broken twigs to the fire, but his focus remained on the mural. His mouth hung open as he worked, and Sonja saw his small nose wriggle with the completion of each line.

When he had finished, the man backed away from the wall and stared at what he had created. The deer's back legs leaned forward, and its front limbs were angled inward to indicate motion. The details of it all astonished Sonja, and she smiled when he looked at her.

Over the course of the previous forty minutes or so, Sonja had decided that painting would likely be the most effective way to communicate. She hesitantly reached for the bowl.

The man looked at her and, at first, seemed reluctant to let her proceed. He only gawked at her suspiciously.

After gentle insistence he relented and pushed the bowl toward his guest. Sonja dipped an index finger into the paint and began her work.

She had decided that a painting of an F.P.U. transport would be pointless. Sonja had never been much of an artist, and she was embarrassed by the fact that this caveman's rendering of a deer was substantially better than what she was about to scrawl onto his otherwise pristine canvas. It seemed there was no other choice, though, so she swathed thin lines with what little steadiness and grace she could foster.

Sonja started with a picture of the sun. It was a clean circle with a spiral that radiated from the center. She added spokes that stretched out in various lengths to indicate rays. Simple stars were added at its edges. Then she created the landscape they now inhabited. It was complete with sloping mountains and trees that stood at different heights.

She fancied it lucid—borderline beautiful—though it scarcely surpassed the elegance of a five year-old's first attempt at finger painting.

The man tilted his head in consideration. As the fire died, he scampered to a corner that was out of sight and returned with more fuel.

She then tried to create a likeness of herself; she even added freckles to the bridge of her hideously disproportionate nose. The man grinned.

Then came her companions. Orion, with his stout features, and Carla with her thin, depleted frame. Lastly she added Eugene, his cropped hair, wiry fingers, and serious jawline creating a hard rectangle on the wall.

The final touch was three broad arrows that pointed downward from the Sun to the stick figure trio that stood on the muddy surface of Earth.

When Sonja was finished, she sighed and leaned back. The man inspected the painting, allowing his left hand to hang in the air just before it.

Then he frowned.

Sonja assumed he didn't understand the implication of the arrows. She extended a finger, pointed to them, and then made a sweeping motion with her palms. His frown deepened. Sonja was unsure of how to react, so she tried to muster a stoic look.

The man backed away. He moved past her and toward the mouth of the cave. When he was close enough to peer out and up into the night sky, he stopped. The man looked up at the stars intently, a fist planted under his chin. Sonja thought of *Le Penseur*—"The Thinker"—the Auguste Rodin sculpture she so adored. She had a tiny version of it on her nightstand back at Headquarters. It had cost her half a year's salary.

Without speaking (what would be the point?) she approached the man and put a hand on his shoulder. He turned his head toward her slightly, but continued to look up into the sky. Something in the distance caused him to back away. He pointed toward the trees, and they were able to ascertain a group of animals scaling the winding trunks.

Eugene had warned her about the Rovers, but she had always had the protection of the Union; she was quite sure they would never purposely harm her. But now things were different. They weren't in Kansas anymore.

She constantly neglected that fact.

With surprising strength, the man grabbed her hand and pulled her back into the cave. They were soon at the area where the impromptu painting had occurred, and the man lifted a large clump of straw matting to reveal an arsenal. Several spears and strange looking tools were arranged neatly on the floor. He picked up three of the instruments and beckoned for her to follow him. He removed more of the matting to reveal a shallow passage that cut through the rear of the cave. At the end of it, she saw the familiar moonlight casting a supernal glow over a dense patch of forest.

Chapter 22

Sonja watched the man move up an embankment and toward her friends.

"Friends." The Board member knew she was taking a multitude of liberties in using that term.

For the first time Sonja noticed how much darker his skin was than her own. He was healthy. Sonja had rotted in space, secluded from her natural environment, confined to the cold metal of a never-ending sequence of cramped transports and rickety biospheres. She examined herself in a puddle, and her lips curled in disgust at her pallid appearance.

Even if she had been alive before the Expansion she knew she wouldn't have protested the Sun harvest. She knew she would've ignored the lack of research preceding the launch of the Pynchon orbiter, and she would, almost certainly, have not been among the throngs of academics who marched against the Energy Extraction Project.

The caveman crouched among the tall weeds; he carefully leveled a spear in his right hand. Lewin saw the Rovers surveying her comrades and was able to fully appreciate the timing of the moment. Had she not volunteered to serve as an intergalactic ambassador she'd be standing in the clearing with them, waiting to be mangled.

Then, with robotic precision, the caveman sprung forward on one heel and hurled his weapon. It reminded her of the sim-vids she had seen of the Olympic games—the contorted stance of the javelin throwers as they sought a flawless trajectory. Now, watching this man do it for real, she understood the accuracy required to land a strike—the skill it took to throw the thing far enough *and* hit an impossibly small target. The spear arched through the night air, its tip whistling only for a moment, before burying itself just below the Rover's ribcage.

When the animal screeched like a scolded dog it caused Sonja to gasp. There was a dark spray and then the hybrid fell, pin-balling against branches until he thumped against the ground below. The man reached for another weapon. Leaning back slightly, he released it with one pronounced shoulder jerk. It spun through the air and blindsided another Rover. There was a dull crack before it slumped and disappeared.

From then on she only observed chaos. The Rovers fled the scene quickly, their ape-like cries ringing through the night. She watched the eyes, seething and bewildered, push through the brush toward the man that had, surprisingly, not raped her.

Even in his startling violence it seemed that he was more gentle and compassionate than anyone she had ever met.

He lowered himself into the tall grass and flattened his body. She knew their eyes were sharp in the dark; she prayed that the man's instincts would rule the day. They scoured the brush for the assailant, barking and lunging erratically. As they drew near, Sonja became nervous.

She reached for a rock that lay at her feet, tested its weight, and pitched it into the darkness. It crashed against a bed of sediment and caused a commotion just loud enough to draw the hybrids' attention. As Sonja watched them pursue the false lead, she realized they had changed. The hybrids possessed the same animal posture, but they were—somehow—more *Sapien*.

They rumbled by her position like a herd of spooked cattle.

When the man emerged from the grove, he was smiling. She returned the look and pointed toward the area where the Rovers had been.

There they observed her motley crew.

"Ad-haum," he muttered, looking directly into her eyes.

It was a gruff word, and Sonja couldn't tell if it had a distinct meaning. It sounded more like a guttural reaction than anything intentional.

He persisted. "Ad-haum."

"Sonja," she replied. There was an awkward moment when she tried to shake his hand.

*   *   *

The criminals started at the man when he approached. None of them could help it. Sonja trailed and said plainly, "He just saved your lives."

Dr. Silvagno stood and walked toward the odd couple. He had forgotten that Sonja was naked, and when she saw him she regained her bearings, blushed and turned.

"Please—my undersuit," she said shyly. Eugene pulled it from a hidden pocket. She stepped into it swiftly and brushed off the patches of soil that were caked to the rear.

"This is..." she started, indicating the man who leaned against a spear, "Adam."

"Adam?" Orion laughed.

"Well, he can't actually speak. Or at least I don't think he can. He's mostly just stared at me. Earlier he made some kind of noise. It sounded like 'Adam.'"

"So you named him that?" Ori asked.

"Yes."

"He's not a pet."

She realized he was right, but she thought that their savior needed a label. They couldn't keep calling him "caveman." Sonja shrugged. "I think he was trying to tell me his name. Back off."

"Should we try and find him an undersuit?" Carla asked wearily.

"Where would we find one?" Eugene chimed in.

"There's actually a few extra on my transport," Sonja replied.

"Will he even want to wear it?"

"Maybe. He seems a little envious."

Adam regarded their vestments with intense scrutiny.

"Fine," Eugene said. "Where's your transport?"

"Only a couple of miles from here."

"Okay. Let's go."

"What about the Rovers?"

Dr. Silvagno peered into the darkness. A rolling fog had scattered the moonlight.

"I think we'll be okay for now," he said finally. "I think your man iced two officers. They'll be working on a new strategy."

*   *   *

When Ori awoke, he saw that Adam was sleeping heavily. His head was against one of the smooth metal support beams of the nav-chair and he was shivering. It was still cold aboard the ship. The option to disable the climate control and open a window had never been a consideration when the thing was designed, so the homeostatic cool remained.

Adam started as if from a vivid dream and scrambled to his feet. He looked around cautiously at the artificial room. The man steered clear of the idly flashing panels and buzzing consoles. They had had a difficult time getting him onboard, and Eugene was opposed to it from the beginning.

"It was stupid of us to send you into that cave in the first place," he said stubbornly, one arm propped against the airlock. "We're supposed to observe and gather information. We're scientists; in this case, anthropologists. We don't interact. *Ever*. I don't know what I was thinking."

"Would you rather be dead?" Sonja was much too casual for his taste. "The hybrids are out there, and they will locate this transport. They're not dumb. And I don't want to make the mistake of assuming that they're not vengeful little bastards. They'll find the cave and wait for him to come back, and then they'll rip him to shreds or inject him with that nifty little concoction. And that'll be it."

He sighed and stuck both hands in his hip pockets. His head was lowered when he began speaking again.

"Fine. This is dangerous, though. You know that. We're screwing around with space-time. The second we entered the atmosphere—the second we stepped on a blade of grass. This is all one big paradox just waiting to blowup in our faces. The butterfly effect—you know?"

"Did you ever consider that maybe this was inevitable? That maybe us being here is *part* of the continuum, and that maybe the world is the way it is (or was) because we *did* come back and exist in this place?"

Eugene inhaled deeply and blinked.

"If we don't take him aboard, he's dead."

"Okay. Fine. Whatever. Bring him in."

When they coaxed him up the ramp he began shaking, even after they had dressed him in a blue undersuit that was much too baggy.

Orion thought of Mayurri; the way she nursed him back to health after he had nearly been beaten to death defending her good name. Ori thought of her thin face and the way she brushed his hair to one side. Following the altercation, she blended his supplements with a multitude of taste-enhancers. She had been gentle when he awoke days after the fight, trembling, his arms folded together tightly.

"I'm so tired of this existence," he had said bitterly. "I'm tired of freezing and having to take pills to survive. I want real food. Fried chicken or asparagus—or something that was at least *living*. I'm human. You're human. We shouldn't have to live like this. It isn't right. It can't be good for us. Look at these!" he yelled, pointing to a mirror and indicating his chipped incisors. "They were made for tearing and chewing, not swallowing capsules. Pills and water; that's it. I don't know how much longer I can take it."

He was embarrassed as soon as he had gotten it all out. Ori barely knew this girl, but he felt the insatiable need to purge himself. He squeezed his eyes shut and tried vainly to conceal the fact that tears streaked his face.

Mayurri rubbed his forehead and kissed him on the cheek.

"I know," she said soothingly.

When she had said those words—those two, seemingly insignificant words—his tremors stopped. His body relaxed and he felt instant relief. Mayurri had given him the strength to keep living even though his brain told him it was pointless.

But now he couldn't stop. Not with her around.

As he watched Adam, Ori tried to think of a way to calm him. He wasn't going to rub his head or whisper sweet nothings (or something as seemingly trite as "I know"), but he did have an idea.

"Hey," he said, startling the man and causing him to perform an awkward about-face. "I know all of this is crazy as hell for you. I really do."

Adam stared at him confusedly. Orion knew the man didn't understand a single word he was saying, just as he didn't understand how anything he'd witnessed was possible. He started to say something else but stopped. The exhausted researcher stood for a moment on weak knees and felt the urge to sleep pull at his eyelids. He started to crawl back onto the cot he had unfolded when he paused. Adam examined his movements, and Ori noted that his shivering had subsided.

Orion nodded. Adam seemed to process the gesture, but you could tell by the look on his face it didn't erase any of the confusion or worry that undoubtedly clouded his primordial gray matter. He mumbled something and slid back down against the wall.

When he thought Orion was asleep, Adam made his way toward Sonja. The caveman eventually dozed off with his back to the researcher.

* * *

When they were all awake it was already late the next morning. They used the nav-system computer to calculate how much time they had until dusk. Everyone but Carla remembered that Earth had a 24-hour day, but none of them knew what time it was currently or when the Sun would set.

They established that there were nine hours left before nightfall.

Sonja handed out supplements to each of the groggy passengers with the exception of Adam. She knew he was hungry, but she decided to wait until they emerged so he could prepare the animal he'd killed. The pills would only add to his confusion.

"Okay," she said triumphantly, pushing the destroyed silver plaque away from her chair with one foot.

"I landed here because there's a beacon nearby. And not just any beacon. It's strong. It's not the Rover ship, and it's not the transport you stole from Headquarters," she said, firing and accusing glance at Eugene.

"I think it's the Borsen engine. I think it did what it was supposed to do and landed near the densest human population it could find."

Everyone exchanged glances and finally Dr. Silvagno spoke up.

"But there's only one person here. He can't be the 'densest human population it could find.'"

"I'm betting there's a large tribe or village somewhere nearby. Nothing else could have prompted the engine to set down where it did."

She was right, and Dr. Silvagno was perturbed that he hadn't realized it sooner. He wrinkled his forehead and rubbed the sandpaper stubble under his chin.

"All right," he said, "So we need to find the ship."

"Does that mean we're going back?" Carla asked in a confused tone.

Sonja didn't say anything.

"If we could, would any of you *really* want to?" Ori said as plainly as possible. There was silence for several minutes as the question hung in the air before them. They were all lost in thought—lost in the infinite possibilities of what using (or not using) the Borsen transporter would mean.

"Maybe we could rig the computer on it... maybe we could end up in a different time."

"No," Sonja said dejectedly. "It doesn't work that way. It's designed to perform a 'hard reverse.' If you tamper with it, the whole thing will shut down and bury its programs in billions of layers of code. We could never hack it. In essence, it means—if the damn thing still works, that is—it would go directly back to our time. Directly back to Headquarters."

Ori squirmed at the thought of leaving. It would be a monumentally stupid decision. After all, this was (quite literally) a dream come true. The idea of being delivered to Union Headquarters with the rest of these fugitives made him even more uncomfortable.

"No matter what we do, we have to find it before the Rovers."

"Agreed," Dr. Silvagno said.

"All right, then," Sonja continued. "Let's get a move on."

She told the computer to open the airlock. It slid up and away and warm air rushed into the bridge of the ship. The Sun was bright and the sky was cloudless. The scent of dandelions and honeysuckle washed over them.

Sonja used the nav-system to pinpoint the location of the beacon. She linked it with the computer in her undersuit and wired the coordinates into the screen of her playback monitor. The computer carried them past Adam's cave. When they neared, he approached the now rotting deer carcass and rushed inside.

"Let's give him a minute," Sonja said in a low voice.

He emerged with a stone blade and skinned the animal with tight, effective strokes. Brushing the flies away, he tore out the meat around the ribs and stuck it in a pouch he had constructed from animal skin. He had started to return to the cave when Sonja stopped him. She tried to explain as best she could that they needed him to come along—that they would be lost without him. He seemed disinterested and had started to gnaw on a sliver of raw flesh. Beaten, she hung her head and examined the playback monitor.

With no other options, she smiled and said, "Thank you."

"Are we going to leave the suit with him?" the doctor squawked.

"Yes. We are." Sonja didn't look at him. "He saved us. It will help keep him warm. Besides, the suit won't last forever. There won't be a trace."

The group moved away from the cave and, when Sonja turned for a final look, she saw that Adam had rekindled his fire. Soon more of the carcass had been stripped and carefully arranged on the bedrock.

Adam watched them leave, and, when they had vanished over a hill, skewered the meat into slabs that could be cured and stored for the harsh winter that lay ahead.

Then he struggled to remove the undersuit.

Chapter 23

The afternoon Sun bore down on them like an angry phoenix. They had all slept, but no one felt rested.

After hours of sullen marching, they finally arrived at the Borsen transporter.

Ori thought that it would be smaller. The ship sat in the center of a steep valley that was lined by firs on every side. It's long, pointed hull had the familiar F.P.U. call signs, and there were numerous airlocks lining the stern. He estimated its length at around two hundred feet.

"Don't look so surprised," Sonja said when she took in his awestruck gaze.

"Did you think it'd be pod-sized? If it worked, we would've used it almost immediately to begin moving to 491. That would take a big ship." She moved closer to the craft and raised one hand.

"There are five levels of seating and a full cafeteria," Sonja continued. "It cost so much to build the damn thing that we could only make one prototype."

"Come on, I'll give you the grand tour."

When they approached the extended ramp, a menacing growl came from behind the massive landing gear.

A slender animal emerged. There were two long, ivory-colored fangs that hung from its upper lip and nearly carved parallel tracks in the Earth as it approached. The thing's head was low and still, and its tail flicked excitedly.

"It's a saber-tooth tiger," Eugene said softly. "They'll be extinct in about twenty thousand years."

"That's comforting," Sonja mused nervously. The giant cat inched toward them, spreading each massive paw leisurely over the arid soil, the muscles in its hindquarters interlocking just below its pelt like steel cogs.

Carla began to tremble, and Orion took her hand. She squeezed it with enough intensity to cause him to wince.

"What are we going to do?" Sonja asked, shooting a terrified glance in Eugene's direction.

"I don't know. These things are endemic only to North and South America. This doesn't make any sense."

Then he noticed something peculiar. A narrow, thimble-sized glob of black fluid hung from the creature's nose. It didn't move like a solid or a liquid—it was more like a plasmatic tentacle, feeling its environment and shimmering reflexively. When the animal took a step, it didn't swing or bob. It just floated, the exposed end periodically winding like a chameleon's tail. Then it retreated into the animal's nostril.

"Jesus," Dr. Silvagno said. "It's him." Ori released Carla's hand and turned to the doctor.

"Him who?"

"Gushkewau'."

"Gushkewau'? What, the *alien* thing? That? It's here?"

"Yes," he said grimly, "It's *in* it."

"What are you talking about?" Sonja blurted in a confused tone.

"I don't have time to explain," he blurted, "But take my word for it: that's not really a cat. Well, it is, but it's more of a... host."

Then the saber-tooth did something none of them had expected. It began floating.

The composition of the entity flowed from the tiger's mouth and encircled the animal's body like a manifestation of the black plague. It was a roiling mist of black obscurity. Soon, the only visible feature of the tiger was its barred canines and green eyes.

"It's controlling him," the doctor said numbly. "How? It couldn't control me..."

"Yes," a deep voice boomed from the thing that resembled a tightly knit swarm of gnats.

Its mouth was shut.

"Creatures in your galaxy are odd; different from most I've encountered. And it has taken me some time to understand, exactly, how your 'nervous system' functions. It's much more complex than I had anticipated. After a decade on that wretched planet I still hadn't fully learned how to control the animals. I could make them eat certain things, mind you, but it was all very menial."

The Sun seemed to bore into them.

"Then you came along. I chipped away at your subconscious for years. I had started to make some progress while you slept. I could make you slap yourself and throw items across your quarters during the return journey. When you awoke,

though, I lost control. It had something to do with that ever-elusive 'human'
element. This 'cat' is different.

"When your life expectancy exceeds two hundred-thousand years, you're
willing to experiment. I have been a prisoner of many worlds—many galaxies, for that
matter—but none quite like this."

The saber-tooth descended and the dark haze dissolved. It shook itself off in
several violent twists and released an unholy roar. Carla covered her ears and
squealed.

"It may take me a little longer to get the hang of the species 'Sapien,'" the
possessed feline hissed, "But I will. I promise. Now that you're here, it will be my
sole occupation."

*   *   *

Orvice was thrown back into his cell once the Ark had touched down. One of
the guards had told him that they were on Earth. The Rover explained everything
that Orion had not: the black hole; the Borsen failure; the second chance.

He wasn't sure whether or not he could trust the hybrid, but it all seemed too
peculiar to be made up. The engines had been powered down for some time and
there was mostly silence.

When Chiu was finally captured she was pumped full of tranquilizers. The
gaping hole she'd created had been double-patched. Orvice listened to the embers
filter down the length of the metal wall, and watched through his rudimentary
peephole as they died on the floor like fatally-wounded fireflies.

When Chiu had regained consciousness, Orvice didn't say anything for a long time. He just stared, wondering if she would be able to see his phosphorescent retinas through the crevice in the wall.

"I know you're there," she finally said after a time. "Your eyes aren't glowing anymore."

"Yes they are. But you can't see them because yours have also made the transition."

Chiu didn't respond.

"It's really not all that bad," Orvice continued in a soft voice. "You'll get used to it."

"The ship isn't moving," she said quizzically. "And I feel too... heavy."

"They've turned the artificial gravity off."

"What do you mean 'off'? If it's off, why do I feel *heavier*?"

"Because we don't need it anymore."

"What are you talking about?"

"We're on Earth."

She was laughing before he had time to offer an explanation.

"*Earth*," she said mockingly. "Go to hell."

Orvice proceeded to lay out everything the guard had communicated to him. Chiu sat in silence as he spoke, producing a bemused smile every now and again, her head leaning to one side as she considered the possibility. When he was finished, she stood and moved toward his voice. He noticed her back had almost completed its arching transformation, and she tried as hard as she could to walk without using her knuckles. Instead, she took on a penguin-hobble, her arms flopping at her sides.

"You don't think he just made it all up?"

"No, I don't. Think about it. You feel heavier. The engines have been turned off. There's not a habitable planet with this kind of gravity within a week of where you were captured."

"So what does this mean?" she asked quietly.

"I don't know. It means we're stuck." He was suddenly filled with rage and proceeded to hammer the metal barrier with his pronounced heels, producing a hollow ring. Chiu was quiet.

"Sorry," he said when the ache in his feet had subsided.

"What will they do with us?" Chiu asked.

Orvice sighed and flattened his palms against his forehead. He smelled horrible. Maybe if they'd given him some powdered soap he wouldn't be so rank. But they wouldn't. They chose to smell like wild animals. He didn't mind the overabundance of hair, the lengthening of his arms, or his comically convex profile. It was the smell. It saturated him and there was no way to be rid of it.

"The treatment isn't over," he said in a matter-of-fact tone. "There's one more injection. It's for your mind."

"What?" she asked cautiously.

"Soon they'll give us both a shot that will enhance our aggressiveness. They say it imbeds new memories. It's got a component that forces your loyalty."

He could hear her begin crying softly as he delivered the news. Orvice wanted to shut up, but he couldn't.

Chiu sniffed and dabbed at her nose.

"They didn't deserve my rebellion."

"Who?"

"The people that were in here with me."

"Hopefully they found a way out."

"I'm sure they did. They're smart. It's just... Carla, you know? The one with dark hair. We've known each other for a long time. We worked the mines together.

"Day and night we'd pull the philidium from the rock and then, when the automatic locks had shut us in for the requisite eight hours, all we could do was talk. She told me about her father. She told me about Friar Grayson; her great, great, great grandfather. She didn't deserve to have her back broken into a million pieces over something that was, at one time, cheered by humanity. She said she used to watch the guards come with supplies. They'd take her dad to the barracks and beat him with chains.

"Sometimes she was forced to watch. They'd usually stop when he turned blue and blood was coming out of his ears. Then they'd give her everything she needed to nurse him back to health. That way he could endure it until he died at a good old age.

"While he recovered her father told her stories about her great grandfather and his house on Mars. He told her about how the atmosphere processors had helped make the cumulous clouds, and how it rained at 3:00 PM every Saturday afternoon.

He told her about a dog—an old chocolate lab—and how it sprinted like it was trying to outrun a tsunami.

"He said that a sandstorm had killed a lot of people in their village."

Chiu dried her eyes and moved away from the hole. The spot of the initial injection in her ribs still ached. She placed a hand over the spot and breathed deeply.

Leaning his head against the metal, Orvice didn't know what to say.

"I guess I flipped because she looked like she didn't need me anymore. I saw her looking at that researcher."

"I'm sure he got her out," Orvice said.

"He better have."

"I'm sure they made it. If they hadn't, wouldn't they be back in here?"

Chiu smiled. She saw his eyes moving in the dark, and they still shone a little. Underneath the animal sheen, there were still hints of blue.

"So what about you? What's your story?"

Orvice was silent for a time.

"It doesn't matter. I did something stupid and here I am. I'd rather have been arrested by the Union."

"Do you think the next shot will be as painful?" she asked hesitantly.

"I don't know. I don't think so."

He knew it would. It was delivered directly to the brain stem.

"Good. I hate pain. I know everyone does, but I really can't take it."

"Me either," he said.

Their doors unlocked simultaneously. Orvice and Chiu were dragged out into the open area in front of their cells. Overhead, the dim green bulb continued its sporadic flicker.

A Rover in a gray undersuit extracted two towering syringes from a broad, black case and fed them a dark fluid. He was much more animated than his comrades.

"We've cashed in our return ticket," he said. "And now we're in need of some attack dogs."

The hybrid meticulously thumped the cylindrical casing.

"This is a special brew. I think you'll like it."

Chiu rolled her head toward Orvice.

"Thanks for listening," she whispered.

"Anytime."

When the needle entered her neck, Chiu felt her mouth widen into an *O*, and was sure that "dog," the word the Rover had used, was entirely the wrong word.

Chapter 24

Orion wondered if anyone had survived the scuttlebug rampage on Europa. The more he thought about it, the less likely it seemed. From what he remembered, the giant worms had demolished everything—even the precious temple that Tryson and his minions had spent years carving out of the primeval permafrost.

His legs were tense and ready to move. He felt the muscles that converged over his kneecaps tighten, aching tediously at the thought of more time spent running.

The saber-tooth-alien-parasite closed in on them.

Without speaking, and almost simultaneously, the group scattered into the surrounding woodland. Dr. Silvagno was the first one to make a run for it. Ori launched into a sprint he didn't think he was capable of. He tore into the thick undergrowth, both hands swinging wildly in front of him as he ripped at branches and the thistly extremities of a vine that extended out in all directions like a green web.

Above the panicked sound of his breathing, he heard, some distance behind him, an earsplitting roar that caused his adrenaline to kick into overdrive. He knew the animal would be on him soon. It was built for this sort of thing.

His heart became a drumming turbine, and he seemed to be making his way through the leaves and clusters of hovering insects with relative ease. A cut just under his left eye had begun to fill with a thin line of blood, but he hadn't noticed. He hadn't processed anything. He just ran.

Then he realized Carla was nowhere to be found.

"Damn it," he muttered to himself and slapped at the offshoots of a small, yellow tree as he passed it. Orion slowed to a jog and finally stopped. He put his hands on his waist and stood there, swallowing the sweet air, trying to conceal a raspy cough from the prowling saber-tooth.

He heard a woodpecker rhythmically boring through the bark of a tree somewhere overhead, and, further into the grove, the sound of dead leaves crackling under the feet of a small mammal. Orion cupped one hand to an ear and strained to locate his companions.

There was nothing; only the sounds of the forest that he had, to his amazement, already grown accustomed to.

Then the bloodcurdling shriek; it echoed through the bramble, and clearly belonged to Carla.

He walked, at a brisk pace, toward the sound. It extended and grew even more sickening. All of the researcher's instincts told him to run, *but*, he thought, *if it is this thing, this Gushkewau', I'll have to confront it eventually. I'll have to fight it sooner or later.*

In front of him the trees spread into a wide *V* and dirty sunlight penetrated the canopy overhead. Carla's voice pleaded.

"Oh God, please," he heard her moan. "Don't do this... please, you don't have to do this!"

A low, rumbling growl shook the humidity.

Finally he was able to see her through the foliage. She lay with her back flat against the ground. The giant cat was crouched over her. His claws slowly lacerated her sides, and blood flowed silently.

Ori froze. He weighed his options and decided to do something rash; as quietly as he could, he leaned over and grasped a fallen tree limb. He tested it with one hand in order to make sure it wasn't the victim of rot. If he was going to hit this thing, he'd have to hit it hard, and he'd have to hit it more than once.

Orion closed in for his attack. Carla was crying softly and her nails cut trenches into the forest floor. The tiger lowered his walrus fangs and dragged them along her chest.

"I don't know you," it said calmly, "But, like most other organisms, you have lived a short life and will die a painful death." The tiger produced an unnatural smile and leaned forward.

With both hands gripping the thick limb, Orion darted over a log and swung as hard as he could. The makeshift club came down on the back of the saber-tooth's head with a tremendous amount of force—so much, in fact, that Ori almost dropped the branch because of the ensuing reverberations. The animal rolled to one side and whined loudly. Carla scrambled away.

The black fog of Gushkewau' seeped out of the animal's ears and spread along the ground. It spiraled momentarily as opaque curls of smoke. The saber-tooth started to get to its feet, and Orion clobbered it again. This time it dropped heavily. He watched the cat's eyes, yellow and wide, roll into its head.

Carla ran to him, gripping her sides, her fingers floating over her shredded undersuit.

"Are you okay?" Orion asked, giving her a once over.

"What do you think?" she said after a stifled laugh. Her lips shook and seemed even more devoid of color than usual.

Ori turned to where she gazed and saw Gushkewau'. It floated just over the debris of the forest floor, seemingly disoriented and trying to regain its bearings.

"Come on," Orion whispered. He took her hand and they ran toward a section of the forest that opened into a grassy clearing. It was a place where they could run, as fast as possible, in the presence of the Sun.

*　　*　　*

Sonja had followed Eugene as closely as she could for half a mile. He was, much to her surprise, in far better shape than herself. The doctor weaved in and out of large brambles without slowing, and minutes later Sonja found herself pleading with him to stop. The doctor lessened his pace and eventually conceded, leaning forward with both hands flat on his knees.

"We should keep moving," he said gruffly. Sonja wiped the sweat from under her nose and licked her lips.

"No," she panted, "Not yet. Give me a second."

Dr. Silvagno frowned and slowed his breathing. He began to pace in tight circles, shaking his wrists and moving his head from side to side like a runner before a meet.

"What if it's already found the others?" she asked.

Eugene closed his eyes and sighed.

"We have no evidence that it caught anyone else."

"I know," she said, "But we should find them. They don't know a damn thing about this place. They need us."

"Since when did you grow a conscience?" he asked in a tone much harsher than he'd intended.

Sonja stared at him coldly.

"Let's get going," she said irritably.

Eugene snorted. They began walking when, just ahead, they saw Orion and Carla come trotting around a bend.

Sonja smiled. She hugged Carla and immediately felt vulnerable. It had been a long time since she'd expressed genuine happiness, and she didn't like that the long-absent proclivity decided to make a comeback in the presence of relative strangers. Even at Headquarters none of the other Board members were what she could honestly label "friends."

The feelings of this particularly shrewd opportunist were usually released as tears and muffled screams that were absorbed by a down pillow that leaned idly against the headboard of her wrought iron bed.

For a moment Sonja retracted her affection, but Carla had already seen it. The inmate returned her embrace.

"How did you get away?" Dr. Silvagno asked in a tone more indicative of a theorist than a concerned cohort.

"I hit him with a stick."

Eugene laughed impatiently and said, "I'm serious."

Orion didn't say anything, and Sonja noticed the jagged virgules ribbing Carla's undersuit. Most of the blood had caked around the edges as a brittle maroon paste.

"Holy hell. Are you okay?" Sonja chirped.

The convict shrugged her shoulders and winced when she accidentally grazed one of the wounds.

It was then that Sonja noticed that the time-traveling space renegades had regained some of the color so distinct of the people alive during the pre-Expansion era. It couldn't be classified as an overnight transformation, but the wan complexion they had always known had started to break.

Dr. Silvagno persisted in his interrogation.

"How did you get away?"

Suddenly filled with contempt, Ori repeated in his most assertive voice, "I told you: I hit him with a stick."

Eugene put on his best Clint Eastwood stare, but the researcher's resolve was unfazed. He appeared to be telling the truth.

"Amazing," he muttered. "Something that complex, that evolved—and it could be beaten with blunt force trauma."

"It's not dead," Orion interrupted. "It left the tiger. It was... stunned," he said thoughtfully, "But it's far from dead."

"I know it's not dead. I didn't mean that. I meant—"

"We need to get back to the Transporter," Sonja interjected. "If it's still alive, then it's looking for us. We shouldn't have stayed still for this long."

"You're right," Eugene concluded, glaring at Orion. "Let's get the hell out of here."

*   *   *

They approached the landing site of the Borsen Transporter just as the Sun had started to sink below the hemline of mountains in the west. Things seemed relatively quiet, and even the screeching birds that had been perched in the treetops all day were lulled into silence by the familiar night chant provided by countless insects.

The surrounding forest cast a dark shadow on the ship. They had waited a long time for a sign of impending hostility, but there was nothing. The Rovers were likely preparing for an assault, but they had to move; there was just enough sunlight left to give the crew cover until they could reach the vessel and secure it from the inside.

After a quick double-check, they concurred that the hideous black fog was nowhere to be seen.

It was now or never.

Sonja moved toward the largest airlock of the ship and quickly tore open the panel covering its entrance computer. She extracted a link from her undersuit and connected it to the playback monitor, which glinted and began running diagnostics. The sky was growing heavy with stars, and she peered past the others and into the darkness at the sound of every creaking bough.

"Could this thing be any slower?" Ori asked no one in particular as he fidgeted with his optic florescent.

"Stop that," Sonja said authoritatively. "If anyone sees that light we're dead."

The darkening Board member commanded the playback monitor to unscramble the ship's entry code.

"What? Unscramble it? You don't have it memorized? You're President of the Union Board, for Christ's sake."

"They never gave it to me," she responded timidly. "And I never asked for it. There was no reason to."

"Yeah," he responded. "I suppose there wasn't."

Sonja rolled her eyes and returned her attention to the monitor. A sequence of fourteen numbers and letter combinations that had to be decoded before the airlock would release. The only reason the ship didn't arm itself and automatically relocate at their attempt to hack it was because of the security clearance assigned to her undersuit's CPU.

Carla bit her tongue, and then, as quietly as she could, whispered, "Look."

They turned toward the tree line in unison.

The familiar eyes burned brightly overhead.

A preternatural frostbite gripped their extremities.

The horde of hybrids emerged from the forest. Some remained positioned in the trees and hills bowling the ship.

"You were lucky before," Fralin shouted. "Tonight will be different."

Sonja cast a sideways glance toward her playback monitor. The red screen reported 18% decryption.

The Rover commander saw the light coming from the tiny screen on her sleeve, and bounded toward her noisily.

"Hoping to go aboard?" he asked delicately. Sonja ripped the connection from the panel and the screen went blank. "Please reconnect cable," the machine said dryly.

The mutant smiled and extended one of his gray hands.

"I'll need your monitor."

Sonja turned to Eugene. She hoped he'd have a plan, but it was obvious he was at a loss. The doctor was too worried about Gushkewau'—too concerned with being overtaken by the mysterious entity yet again. And she couldn't blame him.

Orion and Carla stood quietly, their fingers interlocked, faces downcast.

"Please," Fralin said. "Don't think you can escape. And don't expect your primitive conspirator to save you. It seems he's packed up and moved on."

Fralin moved to her side. "He's smarter than you give him credit for. He identified a threat—something that could snuff out his existence. And he left. He didn't stick around to question it; he followed his gut and decided to setup camp elsewhere. You Union scientists think too much. You should take a lesson from your own kind."

The graying hybrid raised up so that his bulk was at eye-level with the weary humans.

"But it's too late for that. This planet is ours. It will be made in our image."

His mane buzzed with gnats.

Sonja moved away from the airlock.

"The engine doesn't work that way," she said unconvincingly. "There's no going back."

"I was once an engineer; one of your brightest. You hand-picked me from the University. Or don't you remember?"

Sonja released a surprised giggle and then screwed her face in an effort to peer through the matted fur and sphenoidal perversion.

"I developed the concept of the hard reverse; I suggested its implementation into the drive shaft," he said wearily. "This, of course, was before I was sentenced to Pluto.

"Ten years for killing a wanderer because of a telephone. A *telephone*, for God's sake. Is that not the very definition of insanity? Yes, it was a trinket, but it represented so much more—the manifestation of modern communications. I had to have it.

"That's when I realized the futility of it all. We couldn't survive: there was no doubt about it. I understood, too, that I was a part of it: the *disease*.

"I recruited carefully after my release. They understood what the galaxy was coming to, and they helped me develop a way to survive. Some stayed to help me develop the serum. The rest returned to Headquarters."

Fralin narrowed his brilliant eyes and spoke in a low voice.

"They completed their assignment and adjusted the Engine's code. They understood that the only way for us to remedy anything was to be reborn; to return to the beginning."

The doctor stumbled backward with one hand clasped over his mouth. Sonja's eyes were glassy.

"And now I will have my ship."

Fralin turned from her and hobbled back toward a row of officers that brandished polished chain guns.

"Strip them of everything and retrieve the monitor. It's time they encountered the tribe on the other side of the mountain. They will be astonished at where they have come from."

*   *   *

When Ori sat up he pressed his palms against a knot on the back of his head. He held them there and felt his pulse through the pouch of raised flesh. When his eyes had adjusted to the dark, he saw his friends.

They were naked.

So was he.

The landscape below was a muffled blue, but in the faint light of the Moon he could see that it was dotted with small huts. They spread out before him like an earthen washboard, tapering some distance away, eventually concealed by a thin fog that hung over the far hillside.

Orion was unable to see a fire anywhere.

As quietly as he could, he moved from Carla to Sonja, and back to Eugene, waking each of them as gently as possible in turn. Dr. Silvagno groaned, and, like Orion, massaged the back of his head.

"They didn't have to knock us out. What were we going to do? Run for it again?"

Eugene caught Orion's eye, and, with his index finger extended, Ori bought it up to his lips and pointed toward the horizon. Soon, they were all staring coldly at the silent sprawl.

"So the ship had not miscalculated," Sonja whispered proudly.

"It looks that way," Orion responded in a tired voice. He shifted and made an effort to cover himself. The two women, now struck with the same reddening realization, crouched and turned their backs to him.

From below came light footsteps. Before they could locate suitable cover the stunned camaraderie found themselves face to face with a pair of children.

One of them had short hair and appeared mortified at their appearance. He gripped a worn stick tightly, his brown eyes wide and his lips parted just enough to taste the evening air. As the boy leaned in, Ori could see that he was missing some teeth. He was filthy. He had a grotesque potbelly, and, when Ori's eyes had further adjusted to the waning moonlight, he could see the child's sternum moving beneath his skin like an overturned spider.

The other was a young girl, who—surprisingly— had bright red hair and azure eyes.

Sonja noticed her first. The Board member felt as if she were examining a Polaroid from her childhood. This was the first time she had seen another person with a similar genetic makeup outside of a sim-vid. Sonja had done some research during her time at the academy but could never come up with any conclusive evidence as to why the gene for red hair had all but completely disappeared. At the time, it had made her angry.

"Hello," Carla said gently, extending one of her ashy hands. "I'm Carla." The children stepped back, but maintained their observation of the curious strangers.

Her initiative annoyed Dr. Silvango, but even he wasn't sure how to approach them. He managed a smirk. The boy instinctively returned the greeting, revealing a hole where one of his incisors had once stood.

They didn't seem as unkempt as Adam; they weren't clean by any stretch of the imagination, but they appeared, at the very least, have been perfunctorily groomed. Eugene stood and the children backed away cautiously.

Ori, Carla and Sonja followed suit, smiling at the ambassadors and forcing themselves to accept the fact that they weren't clothed. The boy leaned on the twisted branch in his right hand and mouthed something to the girl. She licked her lips in consideration before turning so the strangers could follow.

Animal skin coverings clung to their waists. There was what looked to be a pattern of sinew stitching along the top portion of the garment. They both wore similar outfits—the boy a brown covering, likely removed from a small mammal, and the girl a rudimentary cloth of the same fashion. Hers appeared to have been cut from a slightly larger section of hide.

Soon they were among the thatched housing (which, the doctor noted, were far more advanced than he'd anticipated). They moved between the structures stealthily.

Eugene could see Sonja shared his thoughts—they should run for it. Being here would only further disrupt history, and wandering around a prehistoric, possibly Cro-Magnon campsite in the middle of the night—uninvited by recognized elders—didn't bode well. And it wouldn't look good that all four of them were accompanied by two children that weren't theirs.

They passed a large opening where a fire was dying. Bones were stacked neatly along the charred patch of earth. The smell of roasted flesh wafted to them; it filled their nostrils, and Ori found himself drooling like a Pavlovian dog.

The red-headed girl regarded them once more. Then, without so much as a snort, she disappeared into the maze of structures. The boy, they realized, was nowhere to be found.

After only a few moments the girl had returned, her red curls bouncing in the dark. Behind her was a tall figure; lean and authoritative. He approached cautiously, his eyes alert but still heavy with sleep.

He stopped about ten feet away and said something.

The group looked at each other and remained silent. He came a little closer and repeated his words, which, by their tone, were meant to indicate a question.

Carla saw that the man was older. His hair was gray and the skin on his cheeks sagged like warm wax.

When none of them responded after his second inquiry, he threw his hands angrily toward the low-lying structures that walled them in on all sides.

The child seemed to smooth things over. After hearty protests, the man finally smiled and feigned acceptance. He invited them to move closer.

They did so carefully, following Sonja's lead and keeping their heads slightly bowed.

The elder led them into a hut that was significantly larger than its counterparts. Inside, a small fire blazed. The red-headed girl settled into a nook and crossed her legs, both hands tucked under her chin.

The man indicated that they could sit. He extracted coverings of various sizes from underneath a straw mat, and handed them to each of the strangers. They thanked him eagerly and draped themselves in the rigid fur.

A large, flat, cream-colored animal skin was laid across the dusty floor. The elder called to the girl, and she hopped up, scooted along the side of the hut and returned with a wooden bowl and a handful of a non-descript fruit.

Orion instinctively clicked his tongue, assuming it was food. Sonja understood immediately.

She turned to the old man and extended both hands. He nodded and mumbled something to the girl, who placed the materials before the Union leader.

Her companions watched in amazement as she used the tools to pulverize the fruit into a heavy paste. She then dipped a finger into the substance and scrawled seemingly erratic lines across the prostrate skin.

Sonja had decided to deviate from her cave painting. She concluded that she would have to construct something much more efficient—something both informant and eloquent if she had any hope of truly communicating.

She began by rendering a saber-tooth tiger. She then portrayed her companions, each crouched before the great cat. Moving to the right side of the canvas, she scrawled the image of the newly-discovered village. The homes were flat and ragged; elementary curls of smoke rose from what she hoped looked like ruins. Then she tried her hand at Rovers.

Sonja depicted them as honestly as possible: hunched, covered from head to toe in gray, boorish hair. She was mindful of their inexplicable transformation; their slightly more "human" appearance. She wondered if they would be mistaken for Neanderthals—something that still (she surmised) existed to the west and south of their current location; a variation of these people—of *themselves*, for that matter— that these people had almost certainly encountered.

The cartoon hybrids hurled spears at her friends. They unleashed tigers that went marauding through the village.

The old man leaned back on his earthy cushion and narrowed his eyes. He peered down at the image, the residue from the freshly crushed berries still wet on the stretched canvas. Behind him, the girl with the red-hair sat with her legs crossed, playing with a broken piece of straw, smiling, seemingly oblivious to the warning Sonja was trying to convey.

Cautiously, the man ran his fingers through his beard, eying each of them in turn.

Ori smiled. He hadn't meant to; it was completely involuntary. He was worried that this chief—or whatever he was—might misconstrue its meaning. The researcher was just so damn happy to have interaction with people that hadn't been sentenced to a life spent scavenging among the loathsome Jovian giants.

"Smalog," the elder said daftly, his wrinkled lips curling into an amused grin. "Smalog."

Sonja turned toward Eugene, who only returned the old man's expression and nodded gratefully. Quietly, the red-headed girl in the corner repeated the foreign word. She carelessly retrieved another glossy nettle from the mat she occupied.

Seeing her there, quietly picking at the broken length of straw, Orion couldn't help but think of his faithful little Schultz converter. The way it completed its tasks efficiently; the way it always returned to its storage cube without complaint.

He thought of the way it, like the girl, was completely necessary for his survival.

Smalog.

None of them had a clue what it meant, but they all thought that—for the moment, at least—they had finally caught a break.

Chapter 25

The aroma of roasting meat swam in the cool of morning. Ori nosed his head through the loosely secured entrance of the hut and spotted a hindquarter sizzling in the pre-dawn light.

Across the clearing was the elder from the night before. He sat with several other men, gesticulating somberly with weathered hands, speaking in a throaty jargon that was barely audible.

The elder saw the researcher and left the group of men he'd been conversing with. Nodding, he removed the meat from its spit over the fire and sliced it with a fluted stone.

Upon offering each of them a piece of the kill, there was no hesitation. They reached for the blackened flesh greedily and chewed in silence. When they were full, the man presented them to the council.

The bearded men looked up at the strangers inquisitively. It was clear when they approached that they had been informed of the late night intrusion, but none of them seemed frightened in the least. Instead, one man, younger and with a long scar traversing his neck, displayed a series of paintings that he laid flat against a broad slab of granite.

Sonja saw that her paintings were there, too. These were a response.

She leaned in closely and examined them.

The first image portrayed the village. The skill and accuracy of the artwork solidified her suspicion that she had grossly mislabeled these people as somehow "pre-human." Indeed, like Adam, they seemed, in many ways, to be even more efficient communicators than anyone from her own time.

She saw that they had understood and were prepared to defend the village. In front of the charcoal huts stood a row of tall men, all carrying weapons.

The next painting had renderings of Rovers. In it, they were mangled, their bodies twisted and slain. Sonja was puzzled at the accuracy with which they had depicted the hybrid species they'd only glimpsed through her hurried drawings.

Parallel to this were a series of yellowed skins. Each depicted a bloody conflict with a shorter, more utilitarian foe. The weathered skins stretched out for almost ten yards.

Then it hit her: Homo neanderthalensis. They had mistaken her Rovers for the stout hominids occupying the region beyond the mountains. These people, it appeared, had long been engaged in war.

It was just enough to clarify their intentions. These early sapiens would fight to the death. They would defend Sonja and her friends simply because they were of the same species. It was a reaction she had not expected. Sonja turned her face toward the old man, who studied her reaction intently.

In his eyes she saw the frightening will to defend. It had never occurred to her that these early humans would possess the same ravenous, insatiable desire to protect and guard their terrestrial domain as the final Earth-dwellers. They understood the meaning of *home*.

In 40,000 years, that, apparently, hadn't changed.

By the time the fire had dwindled, the council members were talking sharply with one another. Others began to emerge from their homes. Word of the impending conflict, it seemed, had spread through the village long before sunrise.

Each man carried an array of weapons. Many were duplicates of the spear Adam had so skillfully utilized, and others were heavy tools designed for bludgeoning. Some were completely foreign; they had no presence in the archaeological record and were shaped like boomerangs.

"What's going on?" Dr. Silvagno whispered, poking Sonja in the ribs. "Is it happening *now*?"

"I think so," she said quietly, taking only a second to glance over her shoulder to see if the elder had joined the growing war party.

He had. The lean men of the tribe sharpened their stones and secured their blades with tightly bound lengths of twine. The scene was unsettling, and Carla held fast to Orion.

"I suppose this is the best time," Eugene said matter-of-factly. "The Rovers will be off guard. They won't be able to take the sunlight."

"I don't know," she mused. "They'll probably be in the ship—resting, preparing—but what about the way they've... changed? I don't like it. And how will these people react when they see a Union freighter?"

Orion shrugged. "It's too late now."

"What if they decided to leave? It wouldn't have taken them any more than a few minutes to finish decoding the entry sequence."

"They didn't. You heard the commander. He's operating on some misguided sense of destiny. They aren't going anywhere."

The doctor sighed and started to move away from Sonja. He realized that she had changed.

Still, she had her moments; moments that rekindled memories of his time at the University. Moments where he remembered her fondling the slippery organs of dissected Rovers.

Moments when he could barely move.

Moments when he was petrified.

*   *   *

The Rovers came to them.

The jostling throng had started to move toward the hillside the visitors had descended the night before when the dark figures of their genetically engineered captors appeared at the top of the ridge.

They stood without moving for a time. Each carried a chain gun.

Their transformation was complete. The Rovers were now almost wholly bipedal; their eyes were black, and their hair had receded to reveal a leathery epidermis.

They also seemed perfectly comfortable basking in the presence of the early morning Sun.

"We are here to reclaim Earth," Fralin shouted. "You have rejoined your kind. You are on the precipice of extinction. We are the true ancestors. We will make straight the crooked paths of Man."

"He's insan—"

Carla was cut off by a cry from one of the men that stood at her side. He gasped and clutched at his stomach. Orion saw a thin trail of dark smoke rising from the man's abdomen. In his peripheral, the researcher identified two figures. They skulked in the knee-deep grass rimming the wood-line like lions. Then, with a thunderous howl, the animals plowed through the undergrowth. They were grossly exaggerated Rovers.

Rifles were slung over their backs and jerked violently with the rhythmic bounding of their blitzkrieg.

Their features became more defined the nearer they drew, and Ori found himself staggering backward in horror.

The creatures were familiar. They were Chiu and Orvice.

The tribesman who had been shot fell to his knees, gurgled for a moment, and was dead. The rest of the villagers swarmed around him, mourning loudly. The gravity of the situation soon set in, though, and, mustering their bravado, the legion turned toward their enemy at the hilltop. A cry of rage erupted from the mob, and they moved ahead like a flock of birds, some splitting to the left, some to the right, all converging on the center of the hill as a uniform horde.

The criminals were stunned. To their right, the pair of super-hybrids continued their advance.

Chiu sprung off of a boulder and ripped at a poor contingency that had scarcely begun its charge.

The mutants snarled loudly and dismembered the screaming villagers. Orvice bellowed when a boomerang dug into his scapula. The man who'd flung it stepped away from his victim slowly, clenched his fists, and revealed a serrated blade constructed of bone. It was short but entirely wicked. The enraged Rover moved in on his adversary and delivered a crushing blow. The man slid across the dirt, bellowing in misery and nursing a fractured ankle. Orvice grimaced, crouched, and took on the blurry appearance of a mythical gazelle-ape as he descended on his fallen quarry.

The creature then turned to Sonja. She yelped and tripped over a mound.

The Union Board leader watched in awe as Adam emerged from a scattering of boulders. When the Rover turned toward his enemy, Sonja saw that one of the man's trademark javelins hung like a dart from the small of the hybrid's back.

The animal removed the weapon, broke it over one knee, and quickly cut a path across the low-lying shrubs to where the man knelt.

Adam didn't move.

Time seemed to take on the consistency of molasses. Just when Sonja thought herself able to count the wing beats of a butterfly teasing a nearby tulip, the Rover crashed into the rocks surrounding Adam.

From her position some thirty yards away, she watched as her deliverer removed a wide blade and drove it through the hybrid's neck. There was a gruesome spurt, and it was finished.

Chiu, however, was more strategic.

She circled the band of criminals like a vulture, waiting for a chink in their perimeter to manifest itself. It happened when Ori became tangled with a Rover that had somehow broken the front lines.

The shuddering mutant began working on Carla immediately. The gashes lining her torso were reopened, and the inmate looked like a martyr as she was quickly flayed against the full earth.

Ori had managed to use the hybrid's momentum to vault it, barking madly, onto its back. With one knee straddling the creature's larynx, he picked up a heavy stone and gaveled its head until only a bulbous stump remained.

Then the researcher saw Carla. She kicked like a dreaming dog and swiped lustily at Chiu in a feeble effort to ward off the inevitable.

That's when the doctor lunged atop the ravenous animal, frantically wrapping the full length of his optic florescent around its neck in tight loops.

Chiu immediately turned to Dr. Silvagno, and, like a rabid bull, concentrated all of her energy on bucking this latest inconvenience.

Adam, airborne—spring-loaded—buried his scythe-knife into the hybrid's skull.

The survivors trembled amid the frenzy of dust and gore that settled over the scene.

It was then, after taking a moment to carefully observe the unfolding melee at the base of the ridge, that they realize how oddly the Rovers maneuvered. The hybrids seemed to *swarm* rather than attack with individual consciousness.

A hive mind. The doctor assumed it was yet another unrealized facet of the serum.

Orion covered his ears when the chain guns dug into the teeming battlefield. He had never heard the weapon fired in a place such as this—a place with enough air to create the rattling *boom* that naturally accompanied the sight he had grown accustomed to during his stint on Pluto.

The smell surprised him, too. It was as if a vent of sulfur had unexpectedly split the rock beneath their feet. The villagers took to the surrounding forest when it was apparent they were no match for the thundering weapons. The field spreading out in the shadow of the mountain was littered with bodies—Rover and human alike—though it was obvious the hybrids had dealt greater damage.

Sonja fell into an impromptu depression. It was a hopeless venture, engaging these mutants in hand-to-hand combat. The technology and physical superiority should have told her that from the beginning. Still, there was a persistent *sense*; the will to overcome—something she tritely labeled "hope."

Just as she'd resigned herself to embark on a legendary Twilight binge the second she set foot on the Borsen Transporter, the screams rang out from the trees.

The humans that had survived the initial Rover onslaught unleashed a bevy of flying objects. Spears, the awkwardly fashioned stone boomerangs, revolving clubs; they descended on the paralyzed Rover victory party that had erupted at the epicenter of the massacre.

Some of the hybrids staged a futile retaliation, but the bulk was cut down with staggering accuracy.

The sheer number of projectiles clouded the sky. Ori imagined that it resembled a demonic army of hell-bats that were only seconds away from eviscerating everything in their path.

And, just as quickly as it had begun, the battle was over.

The remaining Rovers scampered into the brush in all directions. That's when Eugene saw Fralin.

He'd survived.

Another cloud appeared, this one infinitely more ominous than the last. It was clear that it wasn't a barrage of primitive-but-lethal instruments of death. The Sun was momentarily eclipsed by a thunderhead that seemed to linger over the pile of dead hybrids. It slowly tapered above the battlefield before charging toward the dumbfounded time travelers.

"It's him. Get to the ship." Eugene was already running when he dropped the bombshell on the group.

Without hesitation they followed suit, scurrying up the steep hillside on all fours.

When he looked over his shoulder, Ori saw the alien fog continue its coalescence as it emerged from the Rovers that were still alive. It was almost too terrible to watch. For a moment, the researcher thought that he was peering into the face of Medusa. He half-expected to turn into a stone representation of his former self. Or, perhaps, be cast into a pillar of salt.

Just as the group crested the slope, the beast turned and split all of its substance between two exhausted Rovers that stood with chain guns poised only fifteen feet away.

They watched numbly as it drained through the animals' eye sockets. It seemed to completely encase the creatures; it seemed to burrow through each and every pore.

Ahead, they saw the Transporter. The ship gleamed strangely in the midday light, its silver hull visible through the green netting reaching branches.

Fralin was already there. His eyes were like saucers, and he backpedaled at the convicts' arrival and trailing storm.

Sonja ripped the playback monitor from his hands, fiddled with it desperately, and managed to link it to the sealed airlock. Seconds later the system reported that the code had been unscrambled successfully.

The portal whisked open and an entry ladder extended.

Without speaking, they hurried onboard.

Fralin followed.

Sonja ran to the nav-system first, initiating its startup programs.

"We need to get off of this planet," she said anxiously.

"Please specify desired coordinates."

"Engines!" Sonja screamed. "Just launch!"

Silence.

"Go!" she shouted. Then, after pausing, added, "Callisto orbit! *Now!*"

The vessel rocketed into the sky.

"Lift-off initiated," the nav-system announced in its soothingly synthetic voice.

Sonja peeled herself from the floor, punched the command to equalize the gravity and moved to the computer that monitored the Borsen engine.

Carla wheezed. She shielded her side, which had begun bleeding again. Ori looked on helplessly, turning frantically from one person to the next. Sonja smiled, accessed a panel, and revealed a case labeled "NANO KIT." She cracked open a vile and millions of repair droids swelled from its mouth. They clustered around Carla's wounds and began working immediately. It looked like ants were consuming her torso.

"Another perk of being on the Board," she said dryly. "Access to prototypical medical technology."

Eugene backed away from the airlock and collapsed onto the floor. Outside, they watched as cumulous clouds hung like gargantuan cotton swabs on the horizon.

"Retraction of landing gear complete," the computer reported.

Then, from around the foyer of the airlock, emerged the pair of possessed hybrids.

Fralin didn't say a word.

The oily presence of Gushkewau' reached out, and then there was darkness.

* * *

Frothy water lapped at the beach. There were hardly any waves, but the tide rose steadily, and the contingency wondered if they were dead.

"I find it odd that just about every one of your species has chosen this location," a voice said. An overweight man in a Hibiscus-pattern shirt stepped out from behind a palmetto. "What is it about this place? Do you find it relaxing?"

The man's stomach hung over a tightly buckled red belt like a sack of flour.

"Who are you?" Carla asked.

"I am that I am."

The man smiled and scratched at his balding scalp. He looked like an oversized Buddha.

"Why are we here?" Fralin seemed to have regained his wits.

"You're here because I'm going to use you. I've finally figured out how to manipulate your species. I still can't identify with this concept of *soul*, but it doesn't matter. The three of you will help me use the Engine so that we can return to our time."

The man continued his diatribe.

"You were right about many things, hybrid commander. Humans are a despicable, uncompromising race."

"My kind is different, Fralin," he said, moving closer to the confused engineer.

"We know what is best for the universe, don't we? Unlike your companions here, you know the truth. And now that I'm here, I'll help you carry out your mission of cleansing your solar system of this... virus."

The fat man smiled, revealing a row of sharp teeth. He moved around Fralin and stood before the weary humans.

Sonja could only think about how delightful a small dose of Twilight would be; how it would shed light on everything.

Chapter 26

The group had regained consciousness, and, after processing their situation, found themselves suspiciously scrutinizing one another in an effort to determine who, exactly, the alien had chosen as its vessel.

"What I'd like you to do," Fralin said, his voice resonating with supernatural authority, "is activate the hard reverse."

Gushkewau' slowly formed an inky turban around the hybrid's head.

Sonja sighed and raised both arms dejectedly. "Fine. But I want you to leave my friends."

The hyrbid laughed and Fralin's eyes flashed brightly against the backdrop of stars that swirled in the porthole.

"No."

Fralin blinked and his neck became rigid. He clawed at his ears and whimpered loudly.

"This 'engineer' is far more valuable than you understand."

The Rover growled and seized her roughly. After opening a small compartment near the airlock, he removed a pair of binders and cuffed her hands and feet. The others didn't fight as the xeno-organism bound each of them in turn.

Then the hybrid commander moved to the Borsen control console and began his work.

Sonja tapped against the metal wall quietly. Her cohorts turned their heads.

To her right was a glass prominence that separated the nav-system from the Engine monitor. It was strangely tinted, and seemed an unnecessary aesthetic more than anything truly functional.

The doctor glanced confusedly between Sonja and the humming pane. Then it hit him.

Plexifab.

"*Twilight,*" Sonja mouthed silently.

For a moment, neither Ori nor Carla understood, but the implication eventually dawned on them.

Pressing against the support beam that jutted out at the joining of floor and wall, the Board member began working on her binders. They were plastic and depressingly durable. It would take time for her to break through the interlocking fibers, and she was afraid the ensuing *snap* would be much too noisy. She kept her eyes focused on Fralin, his sinewy arms punching impatiently at the panel below the nav-system.

The computer rejected every command that was entered into its operating system, but, Sonja realized, that was the point. After an indeterminate number of invalid entries, it would initiate the default defense mechanism—a hard reverse.

Sonja couldn't believe she'd forgotten the security measure. In reality, it didn't take an F.P.U. engineer to activate the hard reverse. It took an idiot. Once Gushkewau' had realized this, he only needed Fralin to input completely random keystrokes.

They didn't have much time.

With each error-ridden directive, the computer's voice grew increasingly stern. It eventually told Fralin that he was allowed only ten more attempts.

By now, all four of the captives were working at their cuffs, and none of them had a clue how they would execute the next move. Their feet were still bound, and, at best, they could dish out an extraordinarily limited assault.

Sonja's binders gave way. The hybrid hadn't heard.

"Only seven more errors allowed before initiation of hard reverse," the computer blurted.

Carla and Orion's binders broke, followed by Eugene's. For a moment, they looked around excitedly, but had the wherewithal to keep their hands behind their backs.

Sonja nudged Dr. Silvagno and looked toward the transparent housing of the Engine's CPU. There, an intersection of finely tuned lasers transmitted the data necessary for the gravity drive to fully engage. Sonja tilted her head toward the processor. She raised her eyebrows excitedly.

"*Hot.*"

The doctor nodded.

Without so much as a "yippee ki-yay!" the Board member sprang to her feet, leveled one elbow, and smashed the plexifab barrier. A waterfall of shimmering particles cascaded to the floor.

"Only five more errors allowed..." the computer stated.

Eugene was already at the processor's junction. He pried the casing open and felt the heat from the fusion cell radiate out and over the ship's bridge.

Sonja rammed her head into Fralin's snout and kneed him in the groin. He cried out, and Gushkewau' erupted from the Rover's mouth.

Orion and Carla brought down the two remaining Rovers easily enough. One had managed to fire a single shot, though it did little more than singe an arbitrary console flashing in a corner of the room. The researcher quickly removed additional binders from the compartment overhead.

Once the hybrids were secure, Ori bolted to Sonja's side next to the collapsed window to help restrain Fralin.

A flame burst out from underneath one of the spiraling chips.

"Warning," the computer said, "Processor temperature approaching unstable threshold."

Eugene collected an especially large section of the shattered plexifab, placed it on the butt of a chain gun, and slid it into the narrow processor housing. The substance began simmering immediately. The doctor tapped his feet and looked like the overwhelmed cook of a brick oven pizzeria.

The doctor then reported an oversight.

"We don't have any capsules."

Sonja turned, and when she did Fralin convulsed, his body bending backward and his chest rippling as if he were the subject of an exorcism.

The familiar black fog rolled across the bridge. Before any of them could react, the creature had wound its way through Sonja's nasal cavity and into each and every one of her nerve endings. She gasped and coughed, knocking over the chair that sat at the nav-system terminal.

A rotating image of Earth appeared on the display as Sonja slammed into an adjacent panel.

"Damn it," Eugene muttered. He withdrew the gun from its oven and precariously balanced the liquid Twilight. Running over to Sonja, he blurted, "I'm sorry, your highness" tilted her head back, and poured the boiling narcotic down her gullet.

Smoke drifted out of her mouth and she gurgled noiselessly.

*   *   *

When Fralin was awoke minutes later, Eugene was standing over him.

"Listen," he said, "I need your help. We need your help."

Fralin surveyed the bridge and saw that Carla and Orion were crouched next to Sonja. She was still alive.

"You know this ship better than anyone, right? There's got to be a margin of error. Shouldn't we be able to adjust the precision of the hard reverse?"

Kneading his head, the Rover stood, and was surprised to find that they had severed his binders. He massaged his wrists and stared at Dr. Silvagno.

"Please," he said. "You have to help us."

Eugene hated that he needed the help of the traitorous mutation, but he didn't see any other alternative. He knew little about the operating systems of transports, and he knew even less about how to hack into the innards of a top-secret Union computer.

Fralin frowned.

"Did she pull him out of me?" He turned to Sonja wearily.

"Yes," Ori said, gently joining the conversation.

"What do you have in mind?"

Dr. Silvagno laid it all out. He quickly explained that after Sonja had absorbed Gushkewau', the Twilight had entered her system and given her control. It was temporary, though. They needed a permanent solution—and they needed it immediately. Leaving the creature here, in this time, wasn't an option.

"We need to return to the post-Expansion system," he said sternly. "But at this specific time." He handed Fralin the playback monitor from Ori's undersuit.

The image on the screen caused Fralin to harden his jaw in contemplation.

After a time, he looked toward Orion. The Rover smiled and cracked his spindly knuckles.

"Yes," he said in a deep voice. "This can be achieved."

Without speaking, the hybrid commander hobbled over to the Borsen computer. He remembered all of the firewalls and security codes that the F.P.U. had hardwired into the system. After a few minutes, he raised his head.

"What the Union failed to fully comprehend is that the Engine can't cross the galaxy *without* traveling through time. It's elementary physics: it's simply the nature of black holes."

"Of course," Dr. Silvagno said absently. "I guess the F.P.U. decided to leave that little tidbit out of the broadcasts."

"Sure they did," Fralin continued. "Why would anyone need to know?"

"Where are we?" the hybrid asked the computer.

"Approaching the Mars-Jupiter Belt."

"Fine," Fralin nodded. "That should be far enough. If anything, we'll draw in a few rocks, but that's it. The margin is hard to identify, you understand. I'll get us as close as I can, but..." he trailed off, "We have to be careful. We can bend the rules. But a fully engaged singularity is designed to self-destruct after one hour."

Dr. Silvagno looked at Sonja. She was sprawled across the rubber-padded floor, with Carla stooping over her, dabbing the sweat from her forehead.

"Okay," he finally said. "It looks like we're only going to get one shot at this."

Some yards away, Ms. Lewin's heart-rate was increasing exponentially.

Chapter 27

"Now," Sonja said, her feet dangling from the edge of a pastel fold-up chair, "that is an interesting take on the situation."

She was back in her favorite spot—just south of the margarita stand, which sat perched on the dune nearest Pier 75. The surf rolled in quietly, waves cresting and breaking with a certain musicality that she hadn't experienced during any of her previous Twilight excursions.

Gushkewau' had reverted back into his original form, and she had learned a lot about him in the past half hour. He was, in a way, humanoid. He had eyes, legs, arms and a nose. But his skin was gelatinous—and, in realizing that, she determined it wasn't really "skin." It was arranged in a pattern not unlike the scales of a snake: still, the stuff was almost feathery. When he became angry, it ruffled and expanded, cloaking his deep, purple eyes.

"I want you to understand," he said as calmly as he could, "What you're doing is pointless. I will overcome this obstacle, just as I have the others."

Sonja sighed and picked up her cocktail, moving the little green, bamboo umbrella out of the way with her tongue. She sipped at it noisily.

"It scares you that I'm in control. Right?" Gushkewau' observed his environment, studying the people that walked past, seemingly oblivious to his plight. "You don't know where they're coming from, do you?"

He backed away from her when she stood. Her sunglasses beamed brightly.

"You know, you're much more attractive this way. I can see why they converted your molecules. That's a punishment I'll have to recommend to Headquarters."

"Your species could never grasp the chemistry behind it," he said arrogantly. "Besides, it's a flawed system. I was able to escape."

Suddenly, he grabbed his feathery cranium and twisted across the sand, his true voice echoing out. It was vibrant and deep—the sound of unobstructed bass. Sonja couldn't interpret it, but she didn't care. She continued probing his brain.

"You escaped," she said finally, "because your world was invaded by a neighboring planet. Yes?" He squealed and red tears flowed from his slanting eyes.

"You escaped when they nearly annihilated your species. A bomb—*a light bomb*," she said, feigning interest, sucking on her straw, "penetrated the holding chamber that kept you and the other prisoners under control. And it ruptured your cell—that was made of... what is that, anyway? Plasma?"

He groaned and carefully found his footing. Sonja dropped the glass she held and clutched at the green umbrella, the stem of which was over one foot in length.

Gushkewau' scowled and she moved closer. Without warning she stuck the sharpened end of the miniature umbrella into his neck. A concentrated arc of blue sprayed across the sand and painted a child that sat constructing a sand castle.

Gushkewau's feathers flared, and he covered his neck with one hand.

"Now," she said, pulling down the brim of her straw hat and looking toward the horizon. "You will learn what fear is."

*   *   *

When the Engine was ignited, it was much the same way as it had been before. There was the pulling, the gravity intensifying and the radiant concentration of light— though, this time, there wasn't quite as much pain. No one was sick when it was over. The hull of the Transporter was built to minimize the effects of the event horizon.

Dr. Silvagno hovered in front of the nav-system, pouring over the menus and drumming the console nervously.

Through the porthole, the doctor saw something he thought he'd never relish; the Sun as he knew it—on its deathbed, red and obese.

"Year and location," he said in a stern voice, when the computer had finished its operations.

"A.E. 621 – October 17th, 13:48."

"Good," Orion said in an exhausted voice, examining his playback monitor. "That gives us about two hours."

"Nice work," Dr. Silvagno said, clapping Fralin on the shoulder. The Rover raised up on his short legs and stared at him. Eugene moved away quietly.

"Okay," he said, "Let's get this piece of junk to Europa."

Once the coordinates were programmed into the computer, the ship barreled off toward Jupiter's frozen moon.

Orion and Carla stood over Sonja. Her sweating had stopped, but the tremors continued.

"How is she?" Dr. Silvagno asked, kneeling next to them. "Not good," Carla said with a sidelong glance. "Look."

She pointed to Sonja's nose, where a dribble of dark blood had begun to leak out and onto the floor of the ship. Eugene turned to Orion, whose lips were drawn together tightly.

"We need to get her into a vaccusuit."

With Fralin's help, they managed to slide her into the thick apparatus. Once her gloves had been attached and her oxygen supply was running, they sat her down in the control chair next to the operating terminal.

"Sixteen minutes until destination," the computer reported.

"Jeez," Ori said after examining the nav-system readout. "Is that thing right? Only sixteen minutes?"

"Yes," Fralin said. "Anti-matter rocket technology; just in case the defaults failed. You wouldn't want a ship full of irate colonists storming the bridge in the event of miss-location."

"I supposed you wouldn't," Orion responded, scratching the wiry beard that had spread across his chin.

Through the porthole, Carla watched as Jupiter grew from a minuscule point of light into the spinning giant she and the rest of the Expansion survivors knew as one of the last stops on the way to nowhere.

"We're almost there," she said, turning to Orion.

"Two minutes until touch down," the computer reported.

The group opened the viewing window and crowded around as the ship approached the frozen surface of Europa. The research site grew larger, and soon the familiar gathering of hovels emerged beyond a glossy plateau.

They stared as the scuttlebugs tore through the surface, collapsing the small Korean issue homes and sending the congregation members fleeing from the Temple. Orion stared in awe as he saw himself, no bigger than a radar blip, climb onboard the supply ship and lift off into the void.

Scuttlebugs piled themselves onto the Temple at the point where the searing round had burned through the surface and penetrated the nest below. Sonja was awake now, and Gushkewau' tried to escape, his black tendrils extending out of her eyes and ears sluggishly. Without a word, Carla lowered the helmet onto Sonja's vaccusuit and clamped it into place. The hissing of the suit's air processor told them they were both sealed inside.

Sonja opened her eyes and looked at Eugene. He put his hand against the plexifab of her visor. She smiled, and her eyes welled with tears.

"Hi," he said softly into her comlink.

"Doctor." She blinked rapidly.

"This was the only way that we could think to—"

"I know," she cut him off, her lips quivering. "Orion's playback monitor. I reviewed it while he was asleep that first night on Earth. This *is* the only way."

Dr. Silvagno smiled and admired her hair. He thought of how she looked on Earth, her figure flawless, as he had always imagined it; her radiant curls clinging to her shoulders and the slender curve of her body against the perfectly white Moon.

"The ship has landed," the computer reported in its monotone voice. "Airlock is secure and ready for exit."

"Thank you," Eugene said before pulling his hand away. Sonja stood, and they saw the flickering black inside her helmet bulging at the suit's hinges. The crew moved into a room adjacent to the bridge and watched through a small, bolt-rimmed porthole as the airlock ran its diagnostics.

Outside, Sonja slid down the ladder, a few of the panicked scuttlebug worshipers trailing her as she leapt over the gaping fissures.

When she entered the Temple, she saw the giant scuttlebugs lying on the surface, their long bodies gyrating as they tried to dig back into their natural environment. The glistening pews had been crushed under their weight, and fantastic flashes of light followed their panicked disappearance.

One of the animals had wedged itself between the pulpit and the altar, its great tusks gaping and struggling to dig into the Europan sludge. Congregation members bowed and chanted in unison, some covered in blood, others lying with their twisted faces exposed to the elements.

Holding her breath, Sonja Lewin charged, flinging herself into the filament-laden mouth of the scuttlebug in the center of the room. The worm's great, purple orifice closed around her, and, in a split-second flash, the animal dissolved into a trail of splintering yellow light.

*   *   *

Soon, the Borsen Transporter had left Europa. Dr. Silvagno had told it to head for Neptune in the off chance that the Headquarters had returned.

No one expected that it had.

Fralin sat quietly in the hangar of the ship, among the levels of seats that wriggled as seatbelts bounced noisily against the plush armrests. Orion entered the room and sat next to him.

"Do you think the Headquarters will be there?"

"No," Fralin said without looking up. "They've already left for 491. I'm certain of that."

"Yeah," Ori said, placing his hands behind his head, "Me too."

Carla walked in and plopped down in the seat across from them. She peered out of the window at Jupiter. The Great Red Spot stared back at her, rotating slowly in the southern hemisphere.

"That's amazing," she said in a hushed voice, drawing in Ori.

He peered out of the small window and saw the Beast staring back at him. It looked, oddly enough, after all these millennia, as if it had finally started to dissipate. He smiled and watched as the planet shrank into obscurity.

"I'll miss it," Carla said softly, looping a dark lock of hair behind one ear. "It really is beautiful."

Sometime later Fralin stood and moved back to the bridge.

"Do you think we'll make it to 491?" she asked Ori, her long eyelashes fluttering.

"Dia," he said. "I've never told anyone, but I've always called it Dia. It corresponds with the numerical designations in the alphabet—you know? And it just sounds... I don't know..." he allowed himself a moment of quiet before continuing. "Alive."

"But who knows if we'll actually make it," he murmured, his countenance fixed on the stellar flurry outside. He placed his hand on hers and absorbed the warmth of her fingers.

"After all," he said, an unexpected smile enlivening his features, "It's only a planet."

Visit www.flowersflix.com for more information regarding videos, books and

other texts.

www.ingramcontent.com/pod-product-compliance
Lightning Source LLC
Chambersburg PA
CBHW032138270626
47172CB00008B/222